Praise for Mackenzie McKade's *Fallon's Revenge*

5 Hearts "…This reviewer can highly recommend Fallon's Revenge to every fan of vampire and cowboy romance. It's one of the best books in this genre that this reviewer has read for a long time."

~ *Danny, Love Romances and More*

4.5 Nymphs "Ms. McKade has crafted an emotionally powerful story… The details in this carefully planned tale, and the sex scenes that will seduce you with their magic, make Fallon's Revenge a fantastic read. This is one you'll not want to miss."

~ *Water Nymph, Literary Nymphs*

5 Shamrocks "Wow! I could sum up my entire review with that one word. I am completely enthralled by Mackenzie McKade's cowboy vampires! …The writing is strong, the plot and subplots are complex yet easy to follow, and both the lead and supporting characters are engaging. This is a book I will definitely be reading again!"

~ *Jennifer, CK2S Kwips and Kritiques*

Fallon's Revenge

Mackenzie McKade

A Samhain Publishing, Ltd. publication.

Samhain Publishing, Ltd.
2932 Ross Clark Circle, #384
Dothan, AL 36301
www.samhainpublishing.com

Fallon's Revenge
Copyright © 2006 by Mackenzie McKade
Print ISBN: 1-59998-340-0
Digital ISBN: 1-59998-179-3

Editing by Angie James
Cover by Scott Carpenter

First Samhain Publishing, Ltd. electronic publication: September 2006
First Samhain Publishing, Ltd. print publication: December 2006

Dedication

To my father who introduced to me the beauty and serenity of the White Mountain Apache Reservation. I love you.

Author's Note

The White Mountain Apache Reservation has been a favorite vacationing spot of mine since I was a child. The beauty of its land and people are truly magnificent. Little was found directly relating to the Apaches living there today. I have used a broad interpretation of Indian ideology. By no means does it accurately reflect the depth of the Apaches' beliefs and traditions.

Chapter One

The sweet, innocent laughter of a child filled Fallon McGregor's head as she took her first breath. The northern Arizona soil cradled her in its arms, holding her like a baby. Again, soft laughter caressed her ears. The unbridled sound warmed her as no fire could in these mountains. It flowed through her veins like the small stream twisting and turning through the valley below.

It was music a mother cherished. A song sung between two connected by birth and love.

She could almost feel Christy's small arms slip around her. Feel her child's breath tickling the hairs at her nape. Fallon's chest rose as she inhaled the powdery scent of baby shampoo her daughter insisted on using even though she had just turned five.

"Mommy, I love you." The words rang through Fallon's head, starting her heart to gently pump one beat, two beats, three…

And then what always followed when Fallon lingered in that dreamscape state, happened.

Christy screamed.

One after another, terrified cries for her mother to save her.

Fallon's heart stopped, her lips parting on a strangled gasp. The breath in her throat caught, as if a fifty pound boulder plunged high from above fell on her chest with a resonant thud. Pain radiated to

...

every extremity. She tried to move her arms—her legs, but they were immobilized. Just like before, she couldn't move—she couldn't save her child.

And then silence.

Always that deathly silence as she came fully awake.

The flutter of Fallon's heart began anew as blood rushed through her veins. She heard the rapid swish, sensed the energy rising, strengthening. Then a great wall of emotion swamped her, threatened to take her under—deeper beneath the sorrow that already paralyzed her.

Tears gathered in her eyes as her naked form burst from the earth, spraying black soil in all directions as she rose into the sky.

"Dammit. I'm alive."

As alive as the undead could be.

Another night had arrived. The strong scent of pines greeted her. A crescent moon, just a sliver in the heavens, was surrounded by stars so bright the sky looked like a picture out of one of Christy's books.

Fallon tried to stop the trembling that shook her. Tried to stop the emotion that rolled down her cheeks, but nothing helped. Nothing would ever stop them, except for the death of her maker—Christy's murderer.

Only then would Fallon let the light of day take her away to join her baby.

"How sick am I when my death is the only thing that can make me happy?" Disheartened, she shook her head.

Pedro Chavez would die slowly beneath her hands. Then she could finally rest.

Still hovering mid-air, Fallon drifted to the ground.

Perhaps her attitude made her reckless and cold. Death she didn't fear. It was life that scared the shit out of her.

Funny how much strength lay in revenge. It was like mainlining a stimulant. Just the thought of Chavez, the one who gave her immortality, heightened her bitterness and need for revenge. She could feel the hot rush of hate grow, building and filling her with a power she never imagined.

Power given to her by her maker—which in turn would lead to Chavez's downfall.

Fallon could do things she never thought possible. Her hearing and eyesight were acute. The magic of the world she had only read about in fairytales or nightmares was hers. She held it at the tips of her fingers, within a thought, a word.

She envisioned a cleansing gust. The wind kicked up, whipping around her body, stroking her nakedness and sending her waist length ebony hair to flutter softly behind her.

She shivered, trying to ease the guilt, the pain—the loneliness. But it was always the same. There was no joy in life without her daughter. Not even the beauty of the night gave her comfort.

"Elements of the earth come to me." Her arms rose as she gazed skyward and waited. Invisible molecules wrapped around her legs, arms, torso and hips. Like always a tickling, almost electric sensation, skittered across her skin as the small particles formed and materialized, outfitting her with clothing of her choice. All she had to do was ask and whatever she wanted, needed, was at her fingertips—except for her baby.

A rumbling inside Fallon's belly brought her palms to her abdomen. Hunger gnawed against her backbone. She hadn't fed in three days. The longest she'd been able to achieve to date. But tonight the effects were wearing on her. She felt lethargic, slow. Even the black leather pants, halter top and boots materializing on her body faded in and out.

Clothes. "Now you see 'em—now you don't." A chuckle rose inside her and then quickly died. *Not a good thing if I am stopping by that little tavern in Pinetop.*

She had arrived in Arizona and went aground not long before the sun began to rise. The small town moved about unaware that a vampire had invaded its territory.

The hand she drew before her eyes and examined was paler and thinner than the night before. Blue veins running up her arm were prominent, as if her skin were tissue paper thin. She knew her slight five-six frame looked delicate, even fragile. But then again, what better way to catch a man than as a helpless woman?

She'd just keep it to herself that she was stronger than any human alive. Being immortal did have some perks, including strength, rapid healing, and never growing older than the age she was at her conversion, twenty-five. But only as long as she took care of her needs.

What she expected to achieve from this self-inflicted torment she wasn't sure, but it saved her from taking what wasn't hers.

Blood.

Fallen pine needles crunched beneath her boots. If she were to hunt down her nemesis, she needed strength. An owl screeched as it landed on a branch of an old oak tree. The bare limbs made her think of long fingers reaching out to grasp her this cloudy September night. She moved slowly away from her resting spot to the sound of flowing water, its tranquility ignored as her pace quickened.

Logically, Fallon knew what she must do. For over a year and a half she'd been able to seduce and take the substances she required to live without killing her prey. Yet, feeding felt like stealing. At least with the exchange of sex she was giving something in return and it fulfilled a need to feel alive. Or at least to touch someone who was.

An ironic laugh parted her lips. "Mom and Dad, you'd roll over in your graves to know what your little girl has become—a prostitute vampire."

"Well, Fallon McGregor, remember nothing is free," her father had always said.

Thinking of a fine mist, her body became that of moisture, tiny drops of dew moving through the trees, fast and silent. It had taken a while to learn this little trick.

Even longer to escape Chavez.

She could still hear his voice, a sensual Spanish accent whispering, "*Mi belleza.*" He called her his beauty.

"Beauty— Bah! The son of a bitch almost drained me of blood."

The night she escaped, Fallon had been so weak Chavez hadn't chained her to the bed. With pure determination, she'd crawled from the house and down a path where a young couple found her. They had offered to help. Their blood had given her much needed strength to run.

"But I won't run forever, Chavez." She had been on the lam for the last six months.

With the thought of the man who had killed her daughter and then taken Fallon as a slave, her blood thickened, unmoving and cold.

Memories of the year under his rule weighed on her. The beatings, the torture, the touch of his hands upon her body, his lips…

Where she should have felt light drifting through the night, she felt burdened, risked falling out of the sky at any moment. Distance was the only thing that weakened his power over her, the only thing that would give her time to learn what she needed to kill him.

She was becoming stronger—smarter.

An elk raised its head skyward as if it could see or hear her. His legs tensed, a slight quiver rattled through them as it prepared to flee. The wild look in the animal's eyes screamed survival.

Fallon knew that feeling.

She also knew in order to succeed—to kill Chavez—she needed a Master, someone to teach her the secrets of the night. It took too long to learn from trial and error. One wrong step and she might end up under Chavez's control again.

She would seek the light of day and perish before that happened.

A gust of air whipped through her misty form, making the particles scatter and then come back together into a stream of moisture as she cut through the night sky. That cute little dark-haired vamp in Oklahoma City had introduced Fallon to her own Master, Lomar. The man had sent Fallon packing the moment she asked, "What could kill a Master vampire?"

Only a Master vampire could teach Fallon what she needed to know. Chavez was centuries older, his power too strong.

"Right now you think you own me—that is if you can catch me. But one day I'll be successful. Both of us will die." The thought eased her mind slightly.

As the tiny drops of dew pulled together, she materialized in the back of a building. The wooden structure looked like it, too, had existed for centuries. The horizontal logs forming the bar looked worn, but glossy as if recently varnished to hide its age. A thread of smoke curled from a stone chimney. She inhaled the pleasing scent of burning pine.

Her hands slid along the sides of her neck, moving upward to fluff her hair and spread it across her shoulders as it streamed down her back. With a twist of her waist, she put a swing to her hips and stepped upon the sidewalk that wrapped around the building and led to the entrance. The parking lot to the side was completely full, vehicles even lined the street in front of the establishment.

From outside she could hear the band tuning up. The hollow sounds of drums, the twang of a steel guitar, and the glide of a bow over a fiddle. A lively tune kicked in, the beat controlling her heart, and for a second quieting the hunger and need inside her. There was a roar of laughter just as she pushed open the door and entered. Immediately, the smell of liquor and stale cigarettes touched her nose and she cringed from the foul odor.

"Damn these heightened senses." She held her breath, but when she released it and sucked in another, the offensive stench overpowered her all over again.

The place was packed.

Cowboys. Men in tight fitting jeans. The posters on the wall announced that a rodeo was in town. Strong, healthy, and virile playmates for tonight's pickin's.

Mmmm… How lucky could she get?

Her body immediately reacted as the tingling of arousal tightened her nipples. A flutter of heat swirled low in her belly. Her mouth salivated as she gazed around the room.

Like it was choreographed, everyone in the place turned their heads and stared at her. Fallon's pulse jumped, sped. When she was alive there was nothing she liked better than a man in a Stetson. And tonight she might even have a couple in her bed—er, their bed. She doubted even one of these studs would like to join her beneath the ground.

The urge to rub her palms together was overwhelming. She felt like she'd entered a candy store.

Wolf-calls and whistles gave her confidence. She had been considered pretty, but there was something about being the undead that worked wonders on a woman. Her hair was fuller and softer, a natural spring to it. Her fingernails were strong and long. Hell, even her breasts were bigger. The thirty-six B she previously sported was now a C cup.

As she sauntered up to the bar the hairs on her neck began to rise as if volts of electricity shimmied across her skin.

Fallon wasn't the only vampire in Pinetop tonight.

For a moment fear raced through her. But the rolling nausea when Chavez was near didn't overwhelm her. No, this was someone else.

She felt him before she saw him. Strong. Masculine. Energy poured off him in waves that filled the room with invisible activity. Hot and alive. Touching and caressing.

He hunted tonight.

His hunger was tentacles of power creeping and searching for prey as they moved throughout the crowd. The gentle probe, teasing and playful, enticed the women and mesmerized the men, masking something dangerous, even deadly.

Whether the vampire came to feed or kill only he knew.

Duh! How could she be so stupid?

Fallon was in the presence of a Master. Authority and control surrounded her. She barely stopped herself from shaking her head with shame. He didn't hunt to feed. He hunted her. She was trespassing.

Primitive and wild, his scent filled Fallon's nostrils. With the intense sensation, she found herself drawn to his magnetism as her gaze followed the shrill laugher and giggles in the corner. Slowly she pivoted on the toes of her boots.

Tall, golden and dangerous was surrounded by a group of women, each praying to win his favor. He stood at least a foot taller than most of the gals. Even with his back to Fallon, she could see the strong tendons in his neck, the tips of wheaten curls from beneath his black Stetson.

"Not now, Lori," he whispered to the brunette at his side, an air of apology in his tone.

Fallon felt his deep, sexy voice slip down her back like liquid silk. Immediately, a warm, wet heat released between her thighs. With just a thought he reached out and stroked her mind, sending shivers up her spine.

Yeah. She might not have recognized who he was immediately, but she knew what he was. They were immortal and could sense when like were around. Not to mention they were open to the telepathic path that all their kindred shared. But she wasn't interested in dealing with a Master right now. There would be questions asked and all she wanted was to feed, perhaps a warm body to lie against, and then she'd be gone.

Before he could speak to her, Fallon threw up a mind block. Pure masculine laughter flowed through her head as he shattered her defenses. He was powerful. Strong. And he was teasing her.

"Great. Just what I needed—a roguish vampire. *Dammit.* I'm not going to get involved with this guy," she whispered to herself. Not even if he made her body burn, and she hadn't even seen his face, only the breadth of those shoulders and that taut, jean-covered ass. The sting in her nipples filtered across her heavy breasts, tightening them to an unbearable ache.

"Puleez," the curvy brunette whined, "dance with me." Her hand stroked invitingly up and down his arm. A handful of other women chimed in that they were next in line to hold him in their arms.

The sensual heat he emitted ensured one, maybe two women, a night of heaven or something more. Fallon refused to consider the outcome, thinking of her own ill fate. You couldn't trust a man with fangs.

This particular vampire wasn't her business, and she had no intentions of getting involved. She'd just have a bite or two of her own and be on her way.

Still, she couldn't seem to look away as her appreciative gaze stroked his broad shoulders. That was until a brawny cowboy lightly touched her arm.

With a whiskey-smooth southern drawl, he asked, "Dance with me?"

A smile slipped across Fallon's face as she stared into eyes the color of rich milk chocolate. Just what she needed—a diversion.

"I'm Mason, pretty lady. Would you like to dance?"

Mason was blond, only a couple inches taller than she. He had the look of an earthy man. One who lived the country life he dressed for in boots, hat, western shirt, and form fitting jeans outlining his—er, goods.

Through shuttered eyes, her gaze fell to the shiny silver belt buckle to stroke the rather impressive bulge between his thighs, again. A bull rider she quickly concluded, judging by his height and build. A pleasant bed partner she assumed, judging by his demeanor and masculinity.

Yes. Mason would do nicely for tonight, and if he had a friend all the better.

Chapter Two

The band playing, the clinking of glasses, laughter, even the ladies surrounding Adrian Trask, were white noise as he focused on one particular woman. The reason he was in Little Tavern tonight. With the coming rodeo a herd of people had arrived, including one unannounced vampiress standing near the bar behind him.

Undead visitors could mean trouble. And trouble was not welcomed on the White Mountain Apache Reservation or Adrian's surrounding towns.

Situated to his left, Lori, a short brunette in an even shorter denim skirt, shifted so that his arm rested against her cotton shirt and between her plump breasts. Her palm slid seductively up and down his arm, drawing his attention. He glanced down into her eyes, touched the brim of his black Stetson, and flashed his warmest smile. Yet his thoughts continued to churn around the objective of his concern.

The unknown vampiress.

He wasn't a parole officer, but it was protocol for the undead passing through another Master's jurisdiction to make their presence known and promise to be on their best behavior.

This particular visitor thought she'd ignore him. Not a smart decision. He was ancient and powerful, over three centuries old. With just a mere thought he could be someone's darkest nightmare.

And she was in his territory now.

With his back to her, he sent energy throughout the room and stroked her mind with a featherlight touch. The unexpected mind block she slung in front of him was entertaining, but useless. Amused laughter tickled the back of his throat as he dissolved the barrier, passing through it as if it were a heavy cloud instead of the solid mass she intended. More for enjoyment than arrogance, he touched her thoughts again, receiving another mental brush off.

Feisty. He chuckled and the corners of his mouth dimpled. His reaction caused a satisfied smirk to pass from Lori to Donna, the blonde situated on his other side. Clearly, Lori felt responsible for his pleasurable response. But she was wrong. His engaging expression had been for the subliminal slap on the hand delivered by the temptress behind him.

It seemed strange that her resistance to acknowledge him or his position of authority didn't anger him. No one defied him. Of course, it wasn't as if he had taken the opportunity to introduce himself—to actually speak with her. It was more an air of indifference she gave off than a lack of respect. She appeared to want to be left alone. But that was never going to happen. He found her intriguing and challenging.

The vampiress had spunk. He could sense her self-confidence, her strength and sexuality, so unlike when she arrived in Pinetop earlier that morning before daybreak. He had known of her arrival. He knew everything. Even more intriguing was the blend of arousal mixing with her air of defiance toward him.

The rich, creamy aroma made his nose rise as he scented her. He inhaled, deeply. *Ahhh...* As he exhaled, his brows pulled together in dismay.

What was it about this temptress?

The female tones around him rose above the music. Two more women joined them, but he heard nothing. Their voices were a buzz, only a murmur. He resisted the urge to brush them from his mind. Which was so unlike him. He'd enjoyed these women before. Hell, he delighted in all members of the softer sex. They were special and deserved respect. But tonight he had only one particular woman on his mind.

Once again he examined his question as his gut clenched tightly. What was it about the vampiress that stirred him, made his cock swell and harden with lust? The roar of blood making a direct path to his groin thundered in his ears. Unbearable pressure built behind his zipper. The need to cup his member was growing into a throbbing ache.

"Now, Adrian? Dance with me, now." Soft and sexy, Lori pleaded with him as the lead guitarist released the final note of the current song they played. He leaned into the microphone and whispered, "Now for a slow one."

"I'm next," Donna chimed, staring up at him through mascara-darkened eyelashes. The statuesque blonde looked inviting decked out in red boots, jeans, and a lacy cowgirl blouse. But she wasn't what he wanted tonight.

Mild amusement touched his lips. "It would be my pleasure, ladies, but not now."

No. At the moment he felt trapped by dark desire. A lust so raw it was painful. It was perplexing that a woman he hadn't even seen could mesmerize him beyond rational thought.

Dammit… Where was his control?

The minute she had entered his territory he had felt shaken. Surprisingly, the land had welcomed her; releasing a sigh as it cradled her within its arms. Almost as if she belonged here.

But she didn't.

By the way she hit town this morning and sought ground she was likely just passing through.

Traveling or running?

With the sun quickly rising in the sky it had been too late to personally introduce himself. Instead he chose to greet her telepathically as she went to ground. Her frantic thoughts as he brushed her mind had torn him from his own resting place. Emotions so desperate and all-consuming clouded her mind. She hadn't even sensed his presence.

He felt hunger clawing at her stomach. The urge to protect her pulled him like a magnet to her side.

But before he could reach her she had already fallen into the sleep of the undead, heart and lungs empty of movement. He had stood over her resting place, listening—hearing nothing.

"Who are you?" he had wondered. "And what are you running from?" Only when his eyes burned and watered, and small, tender blisters rose across his skin as the sun began to rise did he seek his bed.

There was something odd between them that he would have liked to pursue, but he had scented a Master among her essence, a bitter redolence that concerned him. He had yet to mark its owner, but he would.

A crash of a beer bottle as a drunken cowboy pushed from a nearby table jerked him out of his wanderings. A waitress bent to retrieve the shattered glass. "Ouch!" With a tight squeal of surprise, she lunged to her feet holding her hand. "Shit! That hurts."

Mackenzie McKade

Hunger rose inside him. Raw. Primitive. The heady scent of blood, rich and savory, filled his nostrils. His tongue skimmed slowly between his lips. What he would give to lick each of her fingers—one at a time. Mesmerized, he watched the blood flow and then ebb with the pressure she exerted.

"Get her a towel," the bartender yelled.

Upon rising this evening Adrian had fed well to calm the beast the vampiress had awoken in him. But still he felt the creature lifting its head and crying out for more blood—particularly the vampiress's. And the strangest thing was that he could feel her beast reaching out to him, needing to be touched and to feed.

"Adrian?" Lori said.

Damn. Had he missed a question? He caressed the brunette beside him with his gaze. *Such a pretty woman.*

"Yes, darlin'?"

"Let's get out of here." She batted her eyes invitingly.

Lori was ready and willing to be taken, both flesh and blood. The ache in his gums intensified, rivaling that in his jeans. Slowly, his canines begin to push through bone and skin. Donna stepped closer to him so her body touched his, and she gave him a do-you-like-what-you-see look that forced his fangs to explode. The taste of blood filled his mouth and trickled down his throat as his teeth jabbed into the inside of his bottom lip. He would have welcomed the ladies' attention if he hadn't had another on his mind. With a caress of his tongue he coaxed his canines to recede.

"We can make it a threesome," Donna offered. Her thigh rubbed his in a slow up and down motion. A grin creased Lori's mouth as she pressed her body firmly to his. The other women giggled.

22

Someone opened the back door and a cool breeze swept into the room. From where he stood he saw branches bending to the will of Mother Nature. The fresh outdoors clashed against the smoky scent burning in the fireplace as the wind played with the flames. Trees were shadows in the night. Something small and furry scurried across the porch and then the door slammed shut.

"Ladies, I can't think of anyplace I'd rather be, but—"

Unease slithered across his skin as he sensed a man touching the vampiress. Without a further word Adrian broke the grasps the women had on his arms and spun around to see her for the first time, only to watch her glide onto the dance floor with another man.

His hungry gaze slipped over her picture-perfect form. Small and curvy, she wasn't exactly what he expected, not from the feisty defiance he had felt from her previously. No, this woman would bring out a man's need to protect and possess.

"Adrian?" Lori tugged at his shirtsleeve, but he ignored her.

As the cowboy's palm rubbed the vampiress's narrow ribcage and waist, moving across her hip to settle in the small of her back, a deep growl rumbled in Adrian's throat. "Not tonight, buddy. She's mine." An air of jealousy rose unexpectedly within him. He attempted to brush it off, but it only grew as the couple's hips came together and then parted on a turn. Like a dark velvet curtain, her hair rose and settled gently against her body. Adrian felt her light and airy laughter stroke the man with too much intimacy.

He heard the disgruntled breath Lori released beside him. "I thought we were leaving?" Persistently, she pulled on his sleeve.

Donna stepped next to him on the opposite side of where Lori held him in her grip. "My house is closer." She wound her arm through his. "We can go there. C'mon, Adrian."

Not once did he gaze down at them, his vision fixed on the woman moving across the dance floor. "Ladies, excuse me." He pulled from their embrace and, with just a thought, coerced both ladies and the others standing nearby to seek other entertainment. The two cowboys who just walked in would love what the women had in mind tonight.

When finally left alone, Adrian turned his attention back to the dark-haired beauty who intrigued him so. The desperation he had sensed in her when she rose from her resting place this evening was gone. He hadn't been able to stay away from her. Earlier as he hunted he had mentally checked on her. She had been in a terrible state, but now she was completely composed. There was no insecurity or despair in her movements. Instead, a full-frontal seduction campaign was being waged on the dance floor.

She had chosen tonight's victim.

"Over my dead body, darlin'," he whispered beneath his breath.

For several heartbeats, Adrian watched the sway of her hips and wondered what they would feel like beneath him as he parted her legs and drove between them. He had no doubt she would be tight, slipping over him like a glove to hold him in her cradle. As her leather-clad ass moved back and forth, the ache between his thighs grew firmer. His lust became a flame that raced uncontrollably through him.

And damn! She could dance.

Every step was executed to perfection and used to show off her talent. Graceful, light and agile, she moved quickly and easily in and out of the cowboy's arms as they two-stepped across the dance floor. She made the man in her arms look good. The pride on his face said it all. He was the envy of every man, and he knew it.

"Man, what's wrong with me?" Adrian's balls drew tight against the base of his cock. He let the pain wash over him, through him. Just the thought of thrusting in and out of her warm, wet body woke the beast within him. His mouth watered. His canines ached to sink into her slender neck to mark her and make her his. Of course, there was the small problem that she belonged to someone else.

Sonofabitch! He didn't just want her—his body demanded her. He'd have to deal with that little complication later.

She stole every opportunity to press her body against the cowboy's. As her dark, thick eyelashes swept across the top of her cheekbones an expression of pure sensuality greeted the man in her arms each time their eyes met. The woman oozed unadulterated sex appeal. It thickened the air and called to every man in sight, including Adrian.

He pulled his hat from his head, and ran his fingers through his hair before settling his Stetson back into place. "Fuck. Woman, you're killing me." Perspiration beaded his forehead. His pulse raced. His damn heart thumped against his breastbone. For a moment he thought he heard someone call his name. But he was too mesmerized by the scene on the dance floor.

This wasn't like him. He was a Master vampire, not a callow youth. What happened to his control?

With a twist she spun away from the cowboy, her body dissolving into the music as her eyes closed. Her boots and hips moved to the beat. Her shoulders undulated, her breasts pressed tight against the leather halter top. Another movement caused the material to gape and exposed the slightest hint of her rosy areola.

Adrian's mouth salivated. His palms itched to cup her fullness. With a thought he could vanish her clothing. Another thought and he could have her in his bed. He felt weak-kneed as a shiver slid across his skin.

God. He wanted—no—needed to taste her.

Arms raised above her head, her knees bent, taking her body down in a wave. When she raised, her eyelids opened.

Eyes the color of violets met Adrian's, sending his mind into a tailspin. The low, ominous sound that crawled up his throat made her freeze in place, her movements dying along with the music.

His self-control went up in flames as he moved toward her. The beast roared inside him as his fangs emerged. Determination was in his step as his boots clicked against the wooden floor.

"Holy shit!" She choked the words just before he pushed between the cowboy and vampiress and took her into his arms. For a moment he simply drank in her beauty. Her mesmerizing eyes were wide with wonder—or perhaps fear. He didn't know—didn't care. All he knew was it felt right to hold her, to have her body pressed against his.

"I'm cutting in," he shot over a shoulder, as he sent a silent command to the cowboy to seek another beer. At the same time he requested the band to play another slow song. When the music started he trailed one hand to the small of her back, while the other rested beneath her hair. He held her close, and let his body move hers across the floor.

Lilacs. He buried his nose into her hair and inhaled the sweet scent along with the fragrance of her leather clothing. Clothing that suited her small frame. His fingers played unconsciously with the knot of material at her back that kept her halter top in place.

An uneasy huff sent her warm breath to brush his ear. "Uh…you're not thinking of untying that, are you?"

He nuzzled her neck finding the pulse of her life essence. "Not right now, but later…" He scraped his fangs along the blue vein and let the promise of his words linger.

Silence answered him.

"I won't be here later. I'm just passing through." Her voice didn't sharpen, but when he pulled away and looked down at her he could see she meant it.

No way could he let her leave. Not now, not before he discovered what this uncontrollable urge to have her was all about. He had to think of something—quick. "You're hungry. I can't allow you to hurt anyone under my protection."

She stumbled as she crammed her hands between them, palms out, and gave his chest a push. Sharp nails made her point as she poked them into him. A bluish-purple flame sparked in her eyes. Her lips drew back in a silent snarl. "I don't take life."

Relief filtered through him. He attempted to draw her closer, but she held her ground, ducking and slipping from his arms. She was quick, but he was quicker as he caught her arm before she pivoted to leave. He could have sworn she snarled as she spun around and nailed her hot glare at his hand on her biceps. Never removing her withering stare, she jerked, but he held her firmly. "Let. Me. Go," she said between clenched teeth.

She tensed at his touch. Anger moved beneath her skin, hot and fast. Gone was the fun-loving woman. Clearly, she was primed to resist him.

Stupid move. There was no way she could defeat him. Yet, her action earned his respect as he watched for her next move.

The moment her anger flared, so did her hunger.

It was true she had to feed and soon. Her skin was too pale. He would prefer to see the healthy glow he knew would come when she had substance. He sensed her strength waning, she should have been a tad more powerful in attempting to shun his mental probing. Her health was at risk—or another's life.

"I can't let you leave. Not until after you have fed."

A harrumph of disbelief made her chest rise. Her skin was damp with perspiration. His gaze followed a drop of moisture that beaded and fell between her breasts. "I thought you were afraid I'd drain one of your flock of their precious blood," she said beneath her breath. Her tone reflected the tightness in her body.

A hungry vampire was a dangerous vampire—male or female.

Adrian said the only thing he could say, "It is my responsibility to watch over my people. You will feed tonight." His skin felt like it shrank two sizes too small as he continued, "But you will drink from me."

Chapter Three

Fallon couldn't move. Loud and rampant thunder rolled through her head. The powerful vampire holding her hostage on the dance floor as people waltzed around them couldn't possibly have said what she thought she heard.

"You will drink from me."

His words replayed, over and over, in her head as his gaze burned into hers. She blinked once with a deer in the headlight expression she knew had to be plastered on her face. Her tongue quickly slid across dry lips. She swallowed hard, attempting to recover from what he freely offered.

A couple dancing by accidentally bumped her shoulder, causing her to stumble toward him. A whirlwind of emotions whipped through her body. Excitement prickled her skin and sent a shiver up her spine. Her thoughts were short and quick flashes.

One… Masters didn't share their blood with those outside their lineage. Well, unless there were other circumstances involved, as in life or death. It just wasn't heard of.

Ancient blood was powerful.

Two… Chavez's blood had made her immortal and given her strength and power. What results would come from mixing another ancient's essence with her own?

Three… What would be the consequences of a steady diet of one so powerful? Blood, not to mention sex. The idea was heady.

And four… Was he the Master she had been looking for to teach her what she needed to know to kill Chavez?

Holy shit! The intensity of it all slithered beneath her skin. Had she inadvertently stumbled upon just who she was looking for? She felt poised on the edge of a precipice. The possibilities could be immeasurable. She hadn't felt up to dealing with a Master tonight, but there was no way she'd let an opportunity like this pass by.

With all the effort she could muster she tried to hide her excitement. She couldn't reveal what he offered was something she wanted more than life itself. Struggling for composure, she reached deep inside herself and masked her eagerness behind the only other emotion that came so freely nowadays.

Anger.

"Fuck you." She gave her arm a jerk. A futile attempt at freedom as his grasp tightened around her arm.

His eyes darkened. Under a façade of indifference she could smell his arousal. "Later, darlin', but first things first." He was attracted to her. The realization puckered her nipples into taut peaks and sent the most delicious ache down south.

With anger came hunger. The hunger screamed inside her to be fed. It clawed at her insides demanding to be quenched.

It would be so easy for her to give in to him and say, "Okay." But men liked women who played hard to get. And this was a game they were playing, each with their own agenda. What his was, she didn't know—didn't care as long as she met her goal in the end. "Release me and I'll be down the road." She applied an air of resentment, while she screamed silently, *Please. Please. Please. Don't let me go.*

He yanked her against him, his arms snaking around her as their chests and hips crashed into one another. His warm breath brushed across her ear as he said, "It isn't gonna happen, darlin'." *Darlin'* came out a breathy whisper that teased the hairs on her neck. "Even now your hunger is raging, gnawing at your belly. I feel it. It calls to me."

His feet began to move with the rhythm of the slow music. She stumbled for a moment, and then her body melted into his as if they were one person dancing instead of two.

Feel it? Called to him? Fallon was glad he wasn't looking at her to see surprise flicker in her eyes. She knew it had to be there, because that's exactly how she felt—surprised. How the hell could he feel what she was experiencing? But it was true. The beast had overtaken her and something more primitive rose.

She wanted this man—vampire or not.

"This is ridiculous. Just let me go." Her request went unanswered.

His arousal was tight against her abdomen. He didn't try to hide the fact that she affected him. After Chavez, she had made a solemn vow not to get intimately involved with anyone who couldn't walk in the light, but there was something different about the man who held her. She wanted to touch him, feel his body move in and out of hers, his lips on her mouth, her neck, her breasts.

And she didn't even know his name.

Still, the heat of desire burned a path through her.

"Why have you let the hunger rage so long?" His words held a note of disapproval that shocked her. Why would he care? She was no one to him—a stranger.

"It's nothing. I can control it." It was a silly lie. No vampire could fight the hunger.

She gasped, as his fingers slipped through her thick hair, pulling back her head so that her throat arched. Their gazes met, his was condemnatory.

"If you think you control the hunger you're not as smart as I gave you credit for." The firmness in his tone was a reprimand. Then his eyes slid down to the pulse in her throat. His fingertips grazed her hot skin. Immediately, her gut clenched with need. Through heavy lids he glared at her. "Why do you torment yourself?" The softness in his concern didn't hide the invasion he was mounting. She felt his attack straight to her heart.

She closed her eyes, fighting his mental probe for the truth. He dug deeper and deeper into her soul, throwing one barrier aside and then another, quicker than she could throw shields up to stop him. He tore down each wall as if they were paper instead of strong magic. She released a desperate cry as he mentally stripped her naked.

Then something unexpected happened. He withdrew from her mind. Instead of forcing her to his will, he pressed his lips to her ear as they continued to dance across the floor. "Hush, darlin'," he murmured tenderly. "I didn't mean to upset you." His mouth caressed the shell of her ear as he spoke, sending shivers up her back. "When you're ready to talk, I'll be here." His palm smoothed up and down her back.

Tears welled behind her eyelids. What she would give to believe he cared, that she had someone to cling to when memories of Christy rose too harshly for her to bear. But it was a ridiculous thought. The man who held her was a Master and that meant he was also a master of deception.

Fallon laughed the tears from her voice. "Don't hold your breath, buddy." A wave of relief brushed through her as the music ended and he released her. She took an unsteady step backward, feeling strangely bereaved at the loss of his arms around her. "I just need a bite and then I'll be on my way." Her fists went to her hips in a proud stance, when in reality she used it to stop her trembling hands. With a demeanor of confidence, she let her gaze slowly drift over him. "And, I'm a little picky about what I put in my mouth—"

A smile played at the corners of his mouth. Amusement sparkled in his eyes as he cocked a single brow.

Damn. That didn't come out right. She should have said, "—what I eat."

Then as quickly as his amusement appeared it vanished. "This subject is not up for debate. You *will* do what I say." Spoken like a man who was accustomed to getting his way.

Fallon gave a light huff of disbelief, even as she felt success throbbing at her fingertips. *Christy.* Her daughter's name rang in her mind. And for once a glimpse of hope warmed Fallon's heart.

With a mere shrug, she released the air in her lungs. "Then let's get this over so I can be on my way." Cool. Collected. But the hunger inside her was building, crying to be fed and so was the lust that flared when he took her by the hand and headed for the door.

A small spark of fear sliced through her veins. What would happen if she fed then he set her free? Panic came and fled. She couldn't let insecurity steal this opportunity from her. With that thought she knew she'd do anything to stay by his side.

I must be crazy, Adrian thought as he led the mysterious vampiress toward the door. There would be consequences to pay from his actions. The blood link alone was something to consider, and he still hadn't figured out who her Master was. That alone should have given him pause, but it didn't. Of course, he could have just asked her, but his pride held him back.

The chatter in the bar grew louder as the lead guitarist announced a break and the jukebox switched on. Adrian didn't know this woman. She could be someone sent to be his downfall. Another Master seeking his territory, or revenge from someone he had possibly wronged in the centuries he had been undead. The United States had always been his home, so he'd had years to make enemies.

Or was it more elementary? Had she come to steal his heart?

The door made an eerie screech as he opened it and moved aside while holding it wide. With appreciation he watched the gentle sway of her ass as she walked past him.

As they stepped outside, the wind raised her hair and feathered it so it draped her shoulders like a black cape. For a brief moment he worried that she might be cold. But she was immortal. The elements did not affect her as they did humans. She would regulate her temperature to suit.

Still, in her current condition, he knew what the absence of blood did to a body. He had experienced the loss more times than he cared to remember. The numbing sensation of being stuck out in the snow—naked—with no hope of survival. If she wasn't already experiencing the slow, drawn out effects by now, he doubted it would be too much longer before she felt ice cutting through her veins, that heavy ache which made one almost wish for death.

He squeezed her hand in a show of support. Haunting eyes gazed up at him as he led her deeper into the forest that abutted Little Tavern. They met no one because they left by the backdoor and didn't have to pass the parking lot to the side of the building. Pine needles crunched lightly beneath their boots. In the blue-gray moonlight she looked sinfully beautiful. Her hand was small and fragile within his.

Again, a sense of protectiveness rose in him. Why? His attraction to her didn't make sense.

What he offered her was not a wise decision. His blood was powerful. He shared it sparingly and never without justifiable cause. The exchange—and there would be an exchange, he couldn't wait to taste her—would form a blood bond for all time. The link between them would be a tracking mechanism and open up a special mental path between them and through her, possibly, her Master.

Without warning his fangs burst past his gums, the taste of blood in his mouth. He tipped his head and let it flow to the back of his throat, awakening his beast with a roar. Dark and dangerous, it sought out the animal which lay within her.

The feminine reply was sexy as it wrapped around him. He sensed it moving just below her pale skin, teasing and taunting him.

Adrian thought he felt a drop of moisture on his hand. He glanced skyward. Heavy clouds had gathered threatening rain, as they moved into the shadows.

"Where are you taking me?" Her voice was low and throaty, a hint of arousal, but no fear apparent in her question.

And there should have been.

Even in the crowded bar he could have cast a spell to render them invisible or even planted suggestions in the minds of the humans to mask what they saw. For some unknown reason he wanted her to himself, alone. The need to mark her was becoming an obsession and all out crazy because she belonged to another.

He ignored her question and instead he asked, "What is your name, darlin'?"

She cocked her head with a haughty tilt. "Does it matter? You're just a fly-by-night snack for me before I'm on my way."

Rich laughter rolled from his lips. She was going to hold onto her hard-ass act to the bitter end. "A snack? Me?" She had some nerve.

With preternatural speed he pulled her into his arms and they vanished from the wooded area.

When the world stopped churning around him he held her close, his lips a breath away from hers as they stood in the middle of his bedroom. A fire burned in the flagstone fireplace, radiating warmth upon his back. "I plan to make a four-course meal out of you," he murmured, his mouth moving across hers as he spoke. And then he kissed her.

He sipped lightly from her mouth, gliding his tongue along the seams of her full lips. His arms tightened around her as he slanted his head and pressed harder, wanting and needing to get closer. She was soft and pliable beneath his assault. He nipped at her bottom lip and her mouth parted to allow him in.

As his tongue thrust between her lips, her incisors pushed through gum and bone releasing a swirl of blood. Raw hunger sounded, forcing a low timbre from his throat. She tasted of the sweetest honey as he stroked the roof of her mouth and caressed the length of her fangs.

There was nothing sexier than an aroused vampiress. Her taste was an aphrodisiac. Her sensuality could not be compared to that of a mere human. And this particular woman shimmered with sex appeal, an energy Adrian swore wrapped him tightly around her little finger.

But he would never show his hand—at least not yet.

The female whimper that echoed in his mouth stirred his lust like no one had ever done before. Their bodies parted. Both of them were breathing hard, lust burning bright as they stared into each other's eyes.

"Fallon." Her tongue skimmed across her swollen lips as if capturing the last of his kiss. "My name is Fallon McGregor."

Adrian studied her flushed face. She was beautiful.

"Adrian Trask," he shared before taking her mouth once again, because he couldn't stop himself.

Dammit. He couldn't get enough of her. He drank greedily. His fingers played with the knot of leather at her back holding her halter top in place. He needed to see her naked, feel her body beneath his.

She pulled away from him, breaking the kiss. "Whoa, cowboy."

But it was too late. The knot came free in Adrian's hand and the scrap of material floated down her sides, coming to rest between two plump and perky breasts.

Her eyes widened in surprise. Rosy nipples grew into hard pebbles, before his heated stare.

"Remove it," he demanded, unable to take his sight from her beauty.

"But—"

He didn't wait for her denial. "I want you naked, beneath me as you take my blood into your veins and my cock into your body."

"But—"

With a need to see her naked, he willed the material to disappear with a simple thought. The halter top dissolved before his eyes.

She was a tiny thing, but full of attitude.

With a toss of her head she sent her hair over her shoulders, baring her further. A small, tucked waist and curves made to be stroked enticed him. But it was her breasts, which would fit perfectly in his palms, that called to him.

"I don't remember sex being in the deal, cowboy." Her voice was a soft rasp that stirred his blood. "Just a small bite, then I leave—remember?"

No way could she just walk out of his life. Where that thought came from he didn't know. All he knew was for the night, she was his.

"Darlin', I can't let you leave until I've had a taste of you. All of you." He waited a heartbeat for her refusal, a refusal that never came.

Instead, she purred, "Make it quick, lover-boy. I'm on a schedule."

Her futile attempt to appear unmoved by his touch failed miserably when he cupped her breast. She gasped, and he felt the tremor that assailed her. Her eyes darkened. With his heightened sense of smell he breathed in the flood of pheromones she released in response.

Featherlight, his thumb brushed across her taut nipple, back and forth, again and again. "Anything worth doing right should be done nice and..." his other hand pushed beneath her hair and grasped the nape of her neck, "...slow." He drew her head back, baring her throat.

The vein beneath her skin bulged, begging to be taken. Gently, he drew her closer, dipped his head, and ran his tongue over the vessel carrying life to her heart. It pulsed beneath his pursuit, fast little beats which gave her arousal away.

She wanted him.

"Do it," she groaned, her hips brushed against his swollen groin. "Take me, now."

Chapter Four

Surrender was not exactly what Fallon had in mind, even if her body said just the opposite. As she pressed her form against Adrian's hard one, she couldn't believe she'd just asked him to fuck her.

Orange-red flames flickered in the fireplace, matching the burn inside her, as they stood in the middle of his bedroom. Or what she assumed was his bedroom. The transfer from the bar to this new location had her head spinning—or was it the man?

"Ahhh…darlin'. I'm gonna ride you… All. Night. Long." The little growl in his voice sent her mind into a tailspin.

If she put aside the fact that strength and power held her in its grip, how much life could she feel in the arms of someone who had been dead for centuries? Maybe even more? And right now she needed to feel life. Warmth and hope.

His fangs scraped her neck sending prickles across her arms. The vein beneath his tongue throbbed. Hunger exploded. She needed to feel the moment his incisors pierced her skin, the suction of his mouth. She knew it would trigger an orgasm to wash through her body. Not like the rolling of her stomach or the sourness in her throat each time Chavez had touched her.

And she was tired. Tired of running and of the deep, aching loneliness she felt without her daughter.

Perhaps it was because Fallon hadn't fed for days. Maybe her strength, as well as her common sense, was on hiatus, out-to-lunch.

Add to that she was scared. Scared she would end up under Chavez's control once more, Christy's death would never be revenged, or that she had jumped from being one Master's servant to another.

Yet Adrian's touch was unthreatening, gentle, as his tongue teased her throat in slow, sensuous swirls. The firmness of his teeth scraping across her flesh was arousing. He held her tenderly, as if she was a porcelain doll. A thing of beauty to cherish, not a plaything as so many men had made her feel throughout her life—both alive and undead.

And he did feel alive and inviting.

Her skin hummed with sensation as he caressed and squeezed her breast, while kissing each of her eyelids lightly, before pressing his lips to hers.

There was nothing invasive about his touch. He pulled her closer and deepened the kiss. And, God, did he taste good. She compared it to the first time she had sampled Godiva chocolates. Rich. Smooth. Delicious. So exquisite, she had to have another, and then another.

When they parted, her breaths were small pants. She stared into his lust-filled eyes, knowing that tonight would be beyond what she had ever dreamed.

In all honesty, he made her feel vulnerable—strangely like a *real* woman—sexy and desired. No human had ever made her feel that way, even her ex-husband. Just another reason why allowing this vampire to seduce her was a terrible idea.

She was dead—well, undead.

Still, when Adrian called her "darlin'" in that deep, seductive tone, she had to admit to a spark of excitement. His fervor, the promise in his words, stroked an uncontrollable fire inside setting her pulse to speed. Heat swept across her skin. She was achy and hungry to feel his cock between her thighs, parting her wet folds, fucking her hard and fast as she took his blood.

But he had promised nice and slow. The pressure of his hard body rubbing against hers only served to drive her deeper into the dark world of surrender. A seductive takeover she felt too weak to refuse.

She wanted him.

Not only to achieve her goal that always lay in the back of her mind. But something more elemental moved within her.

Desire.

She had felt lust for every man she'd shared a night with, except for Chavez. Yet Adrian did something to her that no one had ever truly done since her transformation. He made her long to believe a future existed as an immortal. That life wasn't just a series of unfortunate events. That she had something to live for.

No. I need to be with Christy.

Mentally, she tried to brush the ridiculous thoughts of a future and living from her head. Okay. This was foolish and extremely dangerous. She had to take control of the situation.

But it was too late.

In a flash they were both naked. Flesh against flesh. Even his boots and cowboy hat vanished.

She whimpered, feeling his hard erection snug against her belly. Her nipples had turned into sensitive nubs. Just the scrape of his chest against hers sent shards of fire through their peaks. She tried to inhale, a weak attempt that only left her breathless.

"Please," she moaned, tossing back her head. Her hair swung across her ass sending chills up her spine. "I need to feel you inside me. Fuck me. Now."

Satisfied male laughter greeted her. "Darlin', I'm gonna fuck you, but first I'll make love to you. Slowly, the way a woman deserves."

Was this man real? Or was his plan to kill her softly?

In a heartbeat he swept her off her feet. She felt small in his arms, feminine, as he carried her to the bed. Gently he laid her down upon the patchwork comforter and he moved away.

The sight made her next breath stick in her throat. It was the first time she had seen him naked, and the man was huge. She wasn't talking about the breadth of his chest, his muscular biceps, or the taut chords that raced through his powerful thighs. His cock was at least eight inches of long, hard pleasure.

The thought of him buried deep inside her released a flood of excitement between her thighs. Her mouth watered to wrap her lips around his firmness, to watch his control vaporize as she took all of him.

From the nightstand by the bed, she watched as he extracted two small ropes.

A sharp spark of apprehension broke the spell he had cast over her. As he turned to gaze at her with darkened eyes, she froze. Surely, he wasn't thinking about tying her to his four-poster bed.

Fallon almost broke into laughter. She was being foolish. A Master vampire didn't need ropes to restrain his victims. His magic was more powerful than any slip of cord. If he wanted to suppress her he could accomplish it with a mere thought. She knew this all too well from experience.

Besides, she was strong enough to break a rope or, with a single thought, cause it to go up in flames.

Still it pleased her that when he touched her mind and felt her anxiety, he whispered, "Trust me."

As he approached, his fangs pressed against his bottom lip. Broad shouldered and lean hipped, he breathed life back into her arousal, stirring the heat of passion to flame anew. If only she could believe the sensual way he smiled at her was for her alone, not just a passing rage of hormones—a one night rodeo.

But trust—never.

And why was she thinking like this? The man was simply a means to an end. Wasn't he? Just someone to teach her what she needed to know to defeat Chavez.

With long, slow swipes, he ran the cool ropes across her breasts. Her nipples drew even tighter so they pulsated with unrelenting hunger. Her globes felt heavy and achy, needing to feel his hands and mouth on them.

At that moment, Fallon knew she would take what she needed from him, and then she'd be gone. The callous thought vanished as his hand circled her wrist.

Intensity like she'd never seen before flared in his eyes, as he drew her arm above her head. He swept over her body with a touch she seemed to feel across every inch of her skin. It tightened each muscle and tendon inside her with anticipation.

"It makes me hot just thinking of you tied to my bed, helpless to my desires." His voice was a mixture of sand and silk across her heightened skin. He inhaled, scenting her and she could have sworn his cock grew even firmer.

The sensual picture of her naked, tied to his bed, and this sexy man posed above her released the most delicious wave of moisture to dampen her thighs.

A moment of silence, then he moved forward and asked, "Would you like me to tie you up?"

His cock jerked, gaining her attention. But it was the heaviness in his voice, the hunger in his gaze that warmed her from the inside out. Her tongue slid between her dry lips. "Yes," she answered before she realized it.

Yes. Yes. Yes. Tie me up and fuck me until the sun rises.

He was true to his promise. Every movement was slow, painfully slow, as he fastened one wrist, and then the other to separate bedposts. His fingertips feathered down the inside of her arm, brushed the swell of one breast, before he traced a line from her waist to her hip. Then he leaned over and lightly blew on her nipple. The sensation was immediate. Sharp stings of fire surged through her breasts, releasing a spasm low in her belly.

"Beautiful," he said before dipping his head and taking her nub into his mouth.

"*Oh…*" Fallon's back arched off the bed, pushing her closer, deeper into his caress. He nipped the hardened peak, and she gasped at the wonderful force shattering in all directions.

"Do you like that?" His voice was warm against her wet skin.

"Oh, God, yes." The words came fast and needy from her trembling lips. "More. Please. More." *More in like spread my thighs, cowboy, and fuck me all night long.*

A rich chuckle surfaced, before he took her other nipple into his mouth. With exquisite pressure he sucked, while kneading her other breast. His tongue made circles around her engorged tip, flicking it several times, making her pull against her constraints.

She wanted to touch him so badly, to feel all that firm muscle beneath her palms, and to hold on to him as he carried her away.

With just a thought she could untie herself. She was dying to weave her fingers through his hair and press him closer to her. But

Fallon had to admit, knowing she couldn't touch him only heightened the depth of her arousal. This was more delicious than she had ever dreamed.

All too soon, he pulled away, sitting up beside her. "Damn, woman, you're sexy." He stroked her with his hot gaze, stopping at the apex of her thighs. His breathing was labored. His nostrils flared. "I need to taste you. Now." The last word came out upon a snarl. The dark, dangerous expression on his face raised the heat in her body.

When he pushed between her legs, spreading her wide, she held her breath. Just the thought of him licking her pussy intimately made her go up in flames.

As he leaned in and ran his tongue across her folds a gush of air burst from her lips, a cry of passion chasing it. Her knees fell apart to give him more access. She raised her hips from the bed, desperately needing him to take her deeper into his mouth. When he clamped down on her clit, drawing it into his mouth, her world tore asunder.

In abandonment, she writhed beneath him. He grasped her hips, holding her still, his mouth and tongue relentless, wringing out her orgasm, forcing her to withstand his assault. Threads of ecstasy ripped from her core, shot up her womb, before rippling to every limb of her body. She tried to hold back the next scream, but couldn't. Her cry only triggered his hunger. A deep, resonant growl surfaced as he went wild sucking and nipping, his tongue driving harder and deeper into her pussy, until she screeched, "Stop. No more. I can't take it."

Then she felt a sharp pain as his fangs pierced the tender skin between her thighs, suddenly releasing another orgasm that shook her from head to toe. Spasm after spasm tightened and released, fast and furious, pushing her mind and body past the point of rational thought and into a place that could only be described as heaven and hell. Her head felt like it was spinning, her body thrown into a mass of sensation.

And then it was gone. A peace like she had never known cradled her. She was floating, a leaf caught in a gentle breeze as she slipped back into reality.

From the vee of her legs, he glanced up through heavy-lidded eyes, a twitch teasing his mouth. Something tightened in her chest. He was drop-dead gorgeous and clearly pleased with himself.

Men.

"My turn." Adrian moved atop her body, gliding his lean, solid chest across her sensitive flesh. With ease he looped his arms beneath the bend of her knees, slowly spreading her thighs wider and raising her hips off the bed.

For what seemed like forever he stared at her slit. Inhaling deeply, a quiet rumble rose in his throat.

In a single thrust he filled her completely.

Fallon groaned with the deep, penetrating sensation. Unable to take her eyes off him, she continued to watch him stare at the juncture where their bodies met.

"God, I knew you'd be hot and tight." He extracted his cock only to pierce her once again. Over and over, slow and forceful, he consumed her body. "Damn, darlin'. Hot. Slick." He sucked in a breath through clenched teeth. "You feel good. So. Damn. Good."

A flush of heat rolled across her skin. Moist perspiration made their bodies slick, the friction building as he pressed close to her. Her inner muscles tightened around him, small contractions that suckled him gently as he rocked into her cradle.

Fallon pulled at her bindings. "Let me go. I need to touch you." As quickly as she could blink she was free. She reached for him. Her long fingernails scraped down his spine.

A tremor shook him. She felt it shimmer through her.

"My turn to taste you," she whispered in his ear.

"I won't last that long if you do," he admitted without shame, as he continued to thrust in and out of her body. His arms quivered. "Fuck, darlin'—" His voice broke. "*Ahhh…*" One last thrust and he ground his hips to hers. His climax triggered another round of spasms to tighten and release inside her.

Fallon opened her mouth, driving her incisors deep into his neck.

Pure unadulterated pleasure flowed through her body as his blood filled her mouth. The coppery scent permeated her nose. The sweet taste draining down her throat as she fed hit her with an impact. Every nerve woke, jittery, as if they would spring from her skin. The power and strength in his blood united with hers. She cried out around his flesh as another climax struck, shaking her to the bones. Even when she was alive, she had never-ever felt anything like this.

She drank and drank, until he murmured, "Fallon, that's enough."

Oh, shit.

With a swipe of her tongue, she closed the pinpricks, sealing away the greatest feed she had ever had. She could still feel the magic that was Adrian flowing through her veins. Energized and happy, she released a contented sigh. The thought made her mentally stumble. Happy? She hadn't felt that emotion in the last year and a half.

Guilt swamped her. She didn't deserve to be happy. Christy certainly wasn't happy.

Adrian felt the moment Fallon pulled away from him. Her body tensed beneath him. She trembled.

Was she upset that he stopped her from feeding?

"I'd better be going." The tightness in her voice scraped across his skin. It grated on his nerves, made him want to reach out and entrap her within his arms.

No way was he letting her leave. He lay, still buried within her body, nuzzled her neck, and then softly kissed her. "Stay with me." His request startled him.

Her eyes squeezed shut. "That wasn't our deal." She swallowed hard, as her eyelids swept open.

"I know." His cock was already hardening as his hips began to rock against her. "I haven't had enough of you."

Uneasy laughter rang in his ear. "You haven't, have you?" Surprise was evident in her uplifted tone.

He gazed into her eyes. "Nah. I don't think I ever will."

She brushed a lock of his hair off his forehead. Her voice softened. "Cowboy, that almost sounded like a proposition."

She was right. It did.

What was wrong with him? She was a stranger, a woman running from something or someone. And what about her Master? He still had not identified who she belonged to.

Mine, whispered through his mind.

The decisive thought rattled him. She wasn't his—never would be. He was only kidding himself if he thought differently. Still he said, "What if it is? Would you stay?"

Man, he just kept digging himself deeper and deeper. But he knew he couldn't let her leave. The woman had wrapped him around her little finger, in a manner of speaking, and there was no trying to argue with the fact.

He wanted her.

His body craved hers.

A shadow crept across her face. She almost looked saddened by his invitation. Then she forced a half-smile that wasn't very convincing. "Sure. Why not?" She shrugged nonchalantly like she could take or leave him. That little bit of knowledge didn't feel real good, especially when she added, "But you have to promise me one thing. You'll let me go when I say it's time. And…you won't probe my memories or read my mind. I'm a solitary person. I enjoy my privacy."

Don't agree with this ultimatum, his conscience screamed. He knew it wasn't wise when he said, "Agreed." For a second he thought the little voice in the back of his head groaned with disapproval. Good sense evaporated in her presence. "Now, where were we?" He wiggled his hips, his erection fully pressed into her tight channel.

Laughter flickered in her eyes. "You were just about to fuck me hard and fast." She writhed beneath him. "Ride me, cowboy."

Chapter Five

The sweet innocent laughter of a child filled Fallon's head as she took her first breath. She lay unmoving, waiting for Christy to say, "Mommy, I love you." When it happened her daughter's voice echoed in her ears.

A tear formed in the corner of Fallon's eye.

As she waited for Christy's scream, the heavy weight of guilt and loneliness swamped Fallon threatening to drag her down into the inky depths of depression. But something was different about tonight. She tried to comprehend the warmth surrounding her.

Chavez?

Fallon felt the claws of fear sink into her mind. She struggled but the arms around her tightened, choking the air from her lungs. Chavez had done this to her before. As she had woken from a nightmare he had given her a sense of peace—of comfort—then jerked it away, allowing the dream to hit her with the force of an avalanche burying her with pain.

Christy screamed in Fallon's mind.

When her daughter's mouth opened again, she heard her own mental voice joining Christy's.

Fallon tried to plunge from the soil. But the arms around her held her deep within the earth.

As she continued to scream in her mind, the dirt layered atop her abruptly exploded upward and then rained down upon her.

She struggled against the hold on her. A deep masculine voice rose above her desperate cries. "Hush, darlin'. It's okay. I'm here."

Still she fought, but it was useless. Her arms and legs were pressed against an unmoving body of stone.

"Open your eyes," the masculine voice demanded, leaving no room for discussion as he pressed her mind with his command to obey.

When her eyes slit open, golden not dark black hair framed a handsome face. She gulped in a gasp of relief. It wasn't Chavez, but Adrian. Last night's events came rushing up to greet her.

Adrian. Not the monster of her nightmares.

She couldn't help throwing her arms around him and holding on.

"Happy to see me?" Although his words were lighthearted, she heard the concern taut in his voice.

She gathered her composure and released him. "Nightmare." A tremor raked her spine.

He frowned. "From your scream it was more than a nightmare."

She didn't want to discuss the dream. Instead she gazed at her surroundings. They rested in a cave. The rich scent of earth surrounded them. Together they lay in a hole some might call a grave. Were they below the house he had brought her to last night or had he whisked her away without her knowledge to another location?

She didn't have time to ponder the thought as the thunder of feet descending the stairs that led to his resting place sounded. All too soon the room filled with strangers. She pressed her naked body close to Adrian as five sets of eyes stared down upon them.

A stern looking man of Indian descent knelt at the edge of where they lay. His hair was as jet black and as long as Fallon's, falling softly over his shoulders as he peered into their shallow grave. Muscular thighs stressed the threads of his blue jeans, showing off the firm bulge between his legs. He wore brushed-leather moccasins that went to his knees. With a touch of his fingers to his straw cowboy hat he greeted Fallon, and then yanked his head in an upward nod. "Boss, what's the problem?"

"No problem, Cougar," Adrian assured him as he drew Fallon closer into his embrace.

A blond-haired man with a cocky grin said, "I'd say we're the problem at the moment." His laughing gaze swept across Fallon's bare hip, following the line of her body until their eyes met. "Ma'am." He caressed the brim of his Stetson like it was a woman. Sensuality seeped from every pore. His boyish good looks cried danger to any woman within his vicinity.

Adrian made a surly sound and a sheet materialized from out of nowhere, covering them both.

The blond man released a stream of hearty laughter. The slender redheaded woman standing next to him poked him hard in the side.

"*Umph*," he groaned. "Maggie?" He tried to embrace her as she swiftly side-stepped him.

"Don't Maggie me, Tucker," she huffed, fire blazing in her green eyes. Her ivory skin was pink with an expression of irritation that spread across her pretty features.

"Baby—"

The endearment earned him another sharp elbow to the ribcage as he closed in on Maggie. Tucker's arms slid around her waist. She squirmed in an attempt to free herself, but Fallon thought her struggle pitifully weak, especially for a vampire. All present were immortal except for the elderly man who nailed her with a grim glare.

"Don't look to me anything's amiss." The man, around seventy, turned his head to the side and spat chewing tobacco on the dirt floor.

Fallon touched his mind. Gary was his name. He was human. Adrian's foreman.

"What's all the caterwauling about?" Gary moved the wad of chew deeper into the pouch of his bottom lip with his tongue, and then rubbed his gray-whiskered chin between his thumb and forefinger. "Women." He turned and stomped away. She could hear his uneven gate move up the stairs.

"Perhaps we have mistaken the situation." A tall, imposing man, western hat pulled low over his dark eyes, looked away. It wasn't a shy, embarrassed movement, but more out of respect. "Boss, do you want me to clear the room?"

From the deep vibration in the man's voice and his large muscular size, Fallon could easily picture this guy as a bouncer. He made an even more imposing vampire. There was an aura of mystery and danger. His confident stance cried don't-mess-with-me-or-else. No one in their right mind would oppose him. She certainly wouldn't.

"Thank you, Briar. If you will give us a moment we'll be upstairs shortly." In a show of possessiveness that surprised her, Adrian tightened his grip around Fallon.

"Let's go." Briar didn't check to see if anyone was following as he headed for the stairs. It further showed his self-assurance that what he commanded would be followed.

Cougar rose. In unison both he and Tucker looked down at Fallon and said, "Ma'am." With their forefinger and thumb, they touched the rim of their hats before stepping away.

From the corner of Fallon's eye she saw Tucker swat Maggie on the ass. She released a small yelp, and then buried her fist into his shoulder.

"Ouch." His cry of pain was riddled with laughter as he rubbed his shoulder. "Wildcat!"

"Whoremonger," she snarled. Her jean-clad hips swayed as she ran after Briar and away from Tucker.

Fallon had one of those "ah-hah" moments as the relationship between Maggie and Tucker became apparent. She wanted him. He wanted anything in a skirt. With the male persuasion that really wasn't something new.

Fallon threw back the sheet. As she began to rise, an arm around her waist pulled her backward. She fell back, twisting so that she laid half on top of Adrian. His delicious erection pressed firmly against her belly.

"Where do you think you're going?" His lips trailed a searing path from her neck down to the swell of one breast. He cupped it lightly in his palm and gently began to knead.

She shrugged. Where was she going? Guess she'd need to figure out where she was before determining where she'd go. He was doing something to her nipple that was driving her crazy and seriously making her reconsider whether leaving was even in her plans.

She arched into his caress and sighed. "Time to get up, isn't it?" But what she wanted was to lose herself in this man.

A smile brightened his handsome features. "Not by my watch." He pinched her nipple, hard.

Crap. A girl couldn't think right lying naked next to a man who was teasing her body into a burning furnace. "What do you have in mind?"

He raised his hips, grinding them against hers. His cock was hard and ready. "Taking you back to bed." His palm smoothed down her hip, until it rested on her ass. "You game?" He squeezed, sending a warm sensation across her skin.

"Oh, yeah. I'm game." Before she finished her sentence they were rising from the ground.

The elements wrapped around her, cleansing and refreshing her skin. The light tingle always made her marvel at how wondrous the untapped magic of the world was. Strange, she could think this way when she wanted so desperately to join her daughter and leave all of this behind.

"You okay?" he asked as their feet touched the ground.

The melancholy that rose within her was hard to hide, but she did her best by changing the subject. "I thought you were taking me back to bed." She raised a brow in question, disappointment softening her voice.

In a heartbeat, he wrapped his arms around her and captured her lips. Unlike last night, which had begun with a gentle exploration, this kiss was fiery and passionate. His tongue pushed beyond her lips, tasting and probing. Their teeth clashed, as she gave as much as she received. His hands moved across her body like a wildfire, leaving her hot and achy.

As the kiss broke, she inhaled sharply. She threw back her head, tossing her black mane behind her. "Fuck me, Adrian."

A solid wall of dirt met her back as he drove her against the cave. She wove her arms around his neck, as he grabbed her thighs and raised her so she could lace her legs around his waist, locking her ankles.

With an upward thrust, his firm erection parted her folds and penetrated her.

"Oh, God," she groaned, loving the fullness inside her.

For a moment they simply gazed into one another's eyes. Then he braced her back against the wall and began to pump in and out of her body, hard and fast. Her heavy breasts bounced with each jab. Her nipples scraping against his chest were raw and sensitive from last night's loving.

"Tight." Voice raspy and strained, he murmured, "So fuckin' hot."

And wet, she wanted to add.

Perched on the edge of orgasm, she tried to modulate her breathing, concentrating and slowing it down. *Inhale—exhale.* She wanted the intensity inside her to last forever. Every nerve ending danced upon a flame of passion.

Adrian buried his head against her shoulder. When his incisors pierced her neck she cried out. Her heart crashed against her chest. Her inner muscles clamped down around him and began to imitate the suction of his mouth, pulling him deeper and deeper as her climax released.

Sparkles of lights flashed behind her closed eyelids. Hunger rose, enhancing the rippling effect inside her. She fought against instinct, holding desire at bay and forcing her canines to retract. She had taken too much of his blood last night and he hadn't yet fed this day. Still her mouth salivated remembering the rush of power she had felt the moment his essence touched her tongue.

With a swipe of his tongue he closed the wound on her neck. He pressed his forehead to hers. "Damn woman. Do you have any idea what you do to me?" His cock was still hard, since he hadn't climaxed. Steadily, he thrust in and out of her pussy. "Unlock your ankles."

When she released the hold her legs had around his waist her feet slid to the ground. He stepped back, extracting himself from her body. There was a moment of emptiness that made her long to feel him deep inside her.

He spun her around to face the dirt wall. "Lean against the wall." With a foot between hers he wedged her legs apart.

Palms braced on the dirt surface, she arched her back. The thought of him taking her from behind sent her mind spinning. She shivered when his strong hands gripped her hips.

"You're beautiful." He struck her ass with the palm of his hand.

A flinch and a startled yip was her reaction as the sting pulsated. Heat radiated through her butt-cheek. And more surprising was that she liked the burn. In fact, it stirred her so that the rumble in her throat almost sounded like a purr of delight.

"Damn, darlin', you have a pretty ass." His fingertips traced the pink imprint of his hand. Everything about this woman made his body swell with the need to feel her wrapped around his cock. Having her poised and ready for him to fuck her from behind was a heady sight, one that sent his heart racing. He leaned into her and buried his cock within her warmth.

"*Ahhh…*" She cried out, arching deeper and giving him better access to move further within her slick pussy. She was wet, so fucking wet—just how he liked his women.

The slap of flesh against flesh, watching their bodies come together as he pumped in and out between her thighs, nearly undid him.

Whack! He couldn't resist landing another hand hard on her sweet ass. Her moan and the way she squirmed beneath his assault made his breathing quicken.

"Do you like your lovin' rough, darlin'?" he snarled through clenched teeth, hoping her answer was yes. Thrust after thrust, he continued to fuck her fast and relentlessly.

In a husky voice, she whispered, "Yes." Her audible pants, short and quick, were arousing. The tendons in her arms drew taut, as she braced herself against the wall and took all he had to give. But what made his balls draw tight against his body was the seductive glance she threw him over her shoulder.

Her hair swung back and forth to frame her beautiful face. Shuttered eyes, her full lips parted on a soft groan. Her incisors had dropped, gleaming sharp and white. She hadn't fed. And by the hungry look in her eyes, she wanted him for breakfast.

A roar started in his head. The fires of hell built in his gut, flaming him into a fever. The rush of blood to his groin was unmerciful, as it slammed into his balls and threatened to rip down his cock. Still he fought back the climax begging to be released.

Her skin was silk beneath his touch. His hand shook as he dragged it across her hip, threading his fingers through her nest of curly hair, before touching her clit.

"*Adrian!*"

A tremor raced through her as his finger circled the engorged bud, once, twice, in steady, fast movements.

Adrian's toes curled in the soft, cool dirt beneath him. The richness of the earth mingled with the spicy scent of their bodies sliding against one another.

"Harder," she cried out, her hips meeting each of his thrusts. Her knees gave a little. His hand on her hip tightened to support her. He pushed in and out, deep and hard, answering her request. At the same time, his thumb and forefinger drew her clit between them and pinched.

Both of their bodies tensed at the same time. One more pump of his hips and he threw back his head and a guttural cry tore from deep within his throat. Her scream of ecstasy joined his, as he held their bodies together and released his seed. Small, jerky movements made him groan. His legs trembled. Every ounce of strength vanished, stripped from him. He leaned forward and collapsed, almost knocking them both over.

With just a thought he carried them to his bedroom. Using the elements he cleansed their bodies, then headed toward the big bed to lay her down. With an air of contentment, he crawled in beside her. She snuggled into him, gazing up at him in an adoring fashion that tightened his chest. The warm, sated smile she gifted him wrapped around his heart.

Through the centuries he had taken many women to his bed, but none who threatened to bring him to his knees like Fallon. What was it about her? What made her different from the others?

He pressed his lips to her forehead. Only then did he hear the noise from outside seeping in through an open window.

A party.

Adrian had forgotten about the rodeo get-together that he and his friends were hosting tonight.

Chapter Six

Through the open door of the kitchen, smells of barbeque sauce and mesquite filled the room. From where she stood just inside, Fallon could see a slab of beef rotating on a spit. The whining and groaning of the motor were uneven as the men near the fire attempted to adjust the weight. When the meat was balanced, the resistance in the engine turned to a soft hum.

Sparks from the flames crackled and danced against the night sky. Shadows rose and fell across the forest background. The weather was crisp, but not cold, as Fallon gazed out at the unpretentious crowd.

Down-home folk. Country people.

Fallon pushed the tips of her fingers into the pockets of her tight jeans, her arms brushing against the gems of the black rhinestone corset she wore.

Yeah. Right. Vampires—country folk?

She stared in disbelief. It all appeared so normal. Tucker, the blond vampire she had met earlier, was flirting with the two women from Little Tavern who had been sidled up to Adrian last night. She remembered Adrian referring to them as Lori and Donna. Just like before each woman was dressed for seduction. Tight blue jeans and low cut shirts showing more than they hid.

Tucker was having little difficulty accepting their attention as he snaked an arm around their shoulders and pulled them tight against him.

Off to the side, Maggie was setting a chocolate cake on a picnic table already laden with food people had evidently brought with them. The redhead's gaze darted to Tucker from time to time. The expression of sorrow on her face saddened Fallon. Tucker was clueless or simply didn't care. Maggie's feelings for the man were obvious, even to Fallon—a stranger.

Laughter rose. The sound of branches snapping beneath a vehicle's tires drew her attention in the direction of a field off in the distance where new arrivals parked. Smiles and greetings abounded as more people pulled up in cars and pickup trucks. It looked like the whole damn town had been invited.

One big happy family.

Just who was Adrian Trask?

After they rose this evening, Adrian scooted her through the house making quick introductions. He had a number of things to look into. In a rush, he kissed her softly and left her in the kitchen to fend for herself, which was a little awkward.

The bubbly little cook Adrian had introduced earlier as Sally said, "You should eat something."

Fallon pulled her hands out of her pockets, palms before her. "No. Thank you. Really, I'm not hungry." It was a lie. She was hungry, but not for the potato salad offered her.

A look of embarrassment that Fallon didn't understand spotted Sally's cheeks, as she set the plate of potato salad down on the large picnic table and continued to bustle about the kitchen. She spoke in perfect English. Yet occasionally she would use her native Apache language to sling orders to her daughter, Susan, across the room. As Sally moved from one plate to another, her coarse black hair, threaded with gray and pulled back in a tight braid, swung from side to side with the rhythm of her full, ankle-length skirt. Comfortable looking moccasins peeked beneath the material.

Susan's skin was like spun milk chocolate, lighter than her mother's, darker than her Caucasian father. Instead of long flowing hair, the younger woman wore it short in a bob. Much like the men she wore jeans and a western shirt, but tennis shoes adorned her feet. There was such a contrast between mother and daughter.

"There's six bedrooms in Adrian's house." Sally freely offered the information as if Fallon had asked. "In addition to the main ranch house, there are various sheds, a barn, a pump house, and four other smaller homes.. Gary, my husband, and I live in one of them. We run the ranch for Adrian during the day."

Gary was the elderly man Fallon had met earlier. Sally's gaze darted to Fallon and then back to the knife she held slicing through a loaf of bread. "Susan and George—"

A boy about the age of three came running through the kitchen. Sally's hand halted the child. He tipped his head up, looking past the wide rim of a cowboy hat two sizes too big. Fallon saw the grin he wore. He was simply adorable dressed like a miniature cowboy, boots and all.

Sally swung him up into her arms. "This little vermin is my grandson, Billy, Susan's boy." Susan stopped washing dishes, pulling her hands from the soapy water and drying them on a towel, as she gazed at her child. A semblance of pride filled her eyes.

He started to squirm, so Sally set the child back on his feet. No sooner than his boots touched the ground he was off again.

"Mom spoils the devil out of my three kids. Roberta and Daniel are older, five and eight." Susan looked toward the picture window that faced the backyard. "The older children must be outside helping their grandpa or getting in his way." As she started putting some of the dishes in the cupboard, Susan continued, "We help Mom and Dad look over the thousand acre ranch during the day for Adrian."

Oh my God! Ding. Ding. Ding. It was finally dawning on Fallon that Sally and her family knew exactly who or more appropriately what Adrian was. And there was no doubt they knew what she was as Fallon remembered the expression on Sally's face when she refused the potato salad.

"George is herding cattle down the mountain. He should be home tomorrow. You'll be able to recognize him. He's a big, shy bear of a man." Susan laughed. "I hope you'll like it here."

Susan said it so sweetly and with such sincerity that all Fallon could do was say, "Thank you."

"Well get on out there and have some fun," Sally encouraged, pulling a pie from the oven.

Fallon wasted no time to escape as she stepped through the open door and leaned momentarily on the hitching post just outside.

Yep! One big happy family. Mortal and immortal. The image of a mouse curled up sleeping in the claws of a cat came to mind, but she brushed the silly thought away.

Christy had been Fallon's only family. Her mother and father perished in a fire when she was a child. No uncles and aunts. No grandparents, except for one grandmother whom Fallon had lived with until she married. After Chavez entered the picture she severed all ties with her last living relative.

Later, after she had escaped Chavez, she visited a library and reviewed microfiche of old newspapers about her and Christy's disappearance. It appeared that her ex had been picked up for their murders. The man had an iron-tight alibi, as usual. Fallon couldn't help wondering whether it was a blonde, brunette, or redhead that supplied his defense. Did he mourn Christy?

In the end, the police had deemed her and Christy victims of foul play, their bodies never discovered.

Chavez had taken so much from her that dreadful night. She pushed away from the hitching post and started to move into the crowd.

Two more vampiresses began to assist Maggie, laying one dish after another on more picnic tables scattered about the open area. There was so much food it looked like they could feed a small country.

Several male vampires she hadn't met were stoking the fire beneath the side of beef. More stood around with drinks in their hands and every once in a while would cast her curious stares.

Okay, so she didn't belong—Fallon knew that—but did they have to make it so obvious?

Sheesh. Once she got the information she needed from Adrian she'd be on her way. She had no desire to disturb the tranquility of their little home. The thought saddened her. Why? Damned if she knew.

Fallon could just imagine the talk her arrival had stirred. It didn't take a brain surgeon to see that Adrian was infatuated with her. Which would make her plans that much easier. But how do you approach the subject of killing someone?

Far off to the right of the cook fire a four-piece band played a lively tune. Before them was a makeshift dance floor, where several couples enjoyed the music as they shuffled hand-in-hand beneath the starry sky. Sawdust was sprinkled lightly on the wood and she could hear the dancers' boots slide when they came in contact with it. Beyond them lay a small stream that rushed across rocks and debris as it cut through Adrian's land.

The couples moving in and out of each other's arms reminded Fallon of her first dance with Adrian in that rustic little tavern in Pinetop. It felt so good to be held in his arms, the soft, sensual music flowing over her, and Adrian bewitching her.

Next she thought of the kiss they'd shared before he left her side to help unload a truck of party supplies. Her lips still tingled with his promise of more where that one came from.

She grinned. If life hadn't dealt her a rotten hand, she could actually see fitting in with all these people, especially Adrian. Where that thought came from she didn't know, and she quickly pushed it away. A man didn't figure into her future plans, because she didn't have a future. The only thing she looked forward to was Chavez's death and joining her daughter.

Several children broke through the crowd, their boisterous laughter teasing her ears as they weaved through the people. With grease lightning speed, they each snatched several cupcakes off the table where Maggie stood.

"Little brats," Maggie chuckled, before she sobered and a tear glistened in her eyes, green eyes that once again looked in Tucker's direction with such sadness and longing.

Damn that man, Fallon thought before she turned her attention back to the noisy children scuffling away with their stolen sweets.

Fallon could see Christy playing with these kids. Fact was her daughter would have loved to have run free amongst the trees and fields of wildflowers. Pain and anger rose within Fallon. She released a heavy sigh, pushing away her emotions and dragging her thoughts from a dream that would never be.

Several more individuals arrived who Fallon remembered seeing at Little Tavern. One of them was the cowboy who had introduced himself as Mason. He stopped to speak to a group of men tapping a keg of beer. A hiss rose and several patted each other on the back for a job well done.

It takes so little to make men happy.

Several bonfires burned brightly. Mason's eyes caught the reflection of the flames, the light flickering in their depths. A man handed him a plastic cup of beer. He blew on the foamy head, sending it from the cup, and then raised the drink to his mouth. Fallon watched his throat muscles work as he swallowed. The pulse of the vein in his neck attracted her like a lodestone.

Quickly, she was overpowered by the rustic scent of blood. The heady swish coursing through his body heightened her hunger. It called to Fallon, as it raced from one artery to the next. The steady beat was mesmerizing.

Damn. She was hungry. Her mouth watered and she couldn't help licking her lips.

In the past, she could ebb the hunger for days at a time, but not today. For some reason she needed to feed—and soon. Every human within her sight became a potential meal. Especially Mason.

She caught his eye and a brilliant smile lit his face. He drew his attention back to the crowd of men, tipped his hat, and then turned to head in her direction. She could hear their rowdy comments and "yeah baby" as he strolled away.

"Don't even think about it." The deep throated warning came from behind her.

She couldn't help the smile that pulled at the corner of her mouth. She glanced over her shoulder to see Adrian directly behind her.

"I feel your hunger." His warm palm closed around her throat. His thumb found her pulse and stroked back and forth, teasingly. Their gazes locked. Her heartbeat doubled at his expert touch. Heat flared through her body. "Let me take care of your need."

"Evenin', Fallon." Fallon drew her sight to the forefront as Mason tipped his hat. He took in her jean-clad legs and the black rhinestone corset she wore. Appreciation gleamed in his eyes. "How about a dance?"

Adrian pressed his hard body to hers. His arms folded around her possessively. "She's mine, cowboy." The firmness in his voice left no doubt he meant what he said.

The grin on Mason's face died a sudden death. "Pardon me," he said, before slipping the rim of his Stetson between his thumb and forefinger. "Fallon." He nodded, then he turned and walked away.

"You will not feed from anyone, but me." The tightness in Adrian's voice was hard to miss.

The happiness Fallon had felt only moments ago vanished. She couldn't help the hurt that seeped into her voice. "You still think I'd hurt one of your people?" With a jerk of her shoulder she tried to escape his grasp, but he held her tightly. Anger simmered below her skin.

Fuck this. In all her days no one had distrusted her. And the one person she wanted—no needed—to trust her clearly didn't.

His warm breath stirred the hair around her ear. "I just like the feel of you sucking on my neck." Her fury fizzled, dying, as he pulled her closer into his embrace. The firm bulge between his thighs pressed against her ass. "Of course, I do like your delicious mouth on other parts of my body." He ground his hips against her.

She turned in his arms and laced her own around his neck. "Mmmm…that does sound good." She pressed her nose to him and nuzzled his neck. He smelled earthy, masculine. Good enough to eat. With a single lick she dragged her tongue over the vein pulsing with life and up his neck and over his jaw, until their lips met in a fiery kiss.

Adrian's large palm pressed against the small of her back, keeping their bodies close. She loved being touched in that sensitive spot. There was something about it that made her feel vulnerable—surrendering to his control. And when a man's hand wasn't there she loved his tongue stroking and caressing the area.

His other palm cupped the back of her head as he slanted his and deepened the kiss. The feel of his tongue invading her mouth brought a fresh rush of desire between her thighs. Her breasts grew heavy. An ache pulsed low in her belly.

A slap on his back jolted them, breaking them apart.

"Feed her." Briar's voice was hoarse and laden. The large man hovered over Fallon. Concern and his own hunger darkened his eyes, barely visible beneath the hat he wore so far down on his forehead.

Fallon immediately got the feeling that she, personally, had done something wrong or incited the crowd of vampires who were all now staring at them. She felt her skin tighten.

"Her hunger is stirring everyone's thirst. Your desire isn't making it any easier on all of us," he complained. "Feed her—fuck her—but whatever you're going to do, do it quickly." The scowl that thinned his lips said that for two cents he'd rip her head off and toss it on the fire. Still she had to admit there was something sexy about him. Briar's cock was a firm ridge beneath the tight blue jeans he wore. And like the man it outlined an impressive package.

Briar raised a brow. His sour expression quickly changed into one of intense satisfaction when he realized exactly where her gaze was directed. He grew even firmer beneath her scrutiny.

Adrian issued a warning with a low, menacing sound.

The heat of embarrassment flooded Fallon's face. Caught like a kid with her hand in the cookie jar. But it was so hard being around all these strong, masculine cowboys and not at least looking. It truly was a woman's candy store.

Fallon wondered whether the blood exchange that she and Adrian had shared had opened a path between her and his people, or was he channeling her emotions through him to them?

She jerked out of Adrian's arms. "I-I'm sorry."

Adrian brushed off the burliness of his friend with a chuckle. He didn't respond to Briar, instead he said, "I'd like to do both, but I think I'd better feed you and then tend to my guests. C'mon." He grasped her trembling hand and led her into the forest, away from others' eyes.

"Maybe I should leave," she said without thought. Pine needles crunched beneath their feet. Darkness surrounded them, but she saw perfectly the little raccoon that peered from behind a bush, and the night owl that blinked in the tree above them.

"Darlin', there's no way I'd let you leave me." He swung her around in his arms. His soft gaze touched her face. "Ignore Briar. His bark is worse than his bite. Besides, it's my fault." His knuckles grazed her cheek. "I should have closed the link between us and them." His lips softly touched hers, moving as he continued to speak, "I wasn't thinking." He captured her mouth in a tender kiss.

Her fingers wadded his cotton shirt as she leaned into him. He tasted so good. The flavor of hops and wheat from a beer he must have drunk touched her taste buds.

And…the man could kiss.

The kiss turned passionate, building quickly into a flame heating her body. It didn't help that he took that moment to slip his hand beneath her corset and fondle an already painful nipple. She whimpered, needing more than a mere caress. She needed him deep within her body touching that part of her which was coiled like a tight spring just waiting to explode.

And, God, she needed to feed. Feel the flow of his blood seep down her throat, quenching the burning hunger inside.

He broke the kiss and slanted his head, baring his throat. "Take me, baby."

Adrian didn't have to ask twice. Her incisors lengthened with his sweet endearment. The piquancy of her own blood filled her mouth. She snuggled close and then sank her fangs deep into his flesh.

The minute she tasted him upon her tongue a surge of energy shook her. Her taste buds were doing the most unusual thing. All she could relate it to was the rock candy she had eaten as a child that exploded in her mouth, popping with multiple flavors. Again, she felt Adrian's power beneath her palms and racing through her veins.

His moan was arousing and another rush of moisture dampened her thighs. But it was nothing like the rich taste of his blood flowing from his body to hers. The coppery scent permeated her nose and the metallic flavor was an aphrodisiac upon her tongue.

"Yes," he groaned. His arms tightened around her.

His hips undulated against hers as he shoved his hand down her pants. Skillful fingers found her slit and pushed between her wet folds.

She inched her feet further apart, loving the sensation of him pumping in and out of her pussy as she fed. When he circled her clit it felt like a Roman candle exploded inside her. She gasped, breaking the suction on his throat. She cried out as her head lolled back. Wave after wave of sensations rippled over her. If he hadn't held her she would have collapsed.

"Close the incisions, darlin'."

Oh shit! She tried to gather her wits long enough to staunch the two streams of blood oozing from the puncture wounds. With a swiped her tongue across the bite marks, she watched the skin heal and mend.

The pulse between her legs still throbbed, as his hand lay against her swollen folds. "I'm so sorry." But her orgasm had erupted without any warning. One minute she was feeding, the next writhing in his arms.

He extracted his hand, pulling her closer within his embrace. "No apologies. You're beautiful, hot and passionate." She pushed her hand between them, intent on cupping his erection. She startled, as he stepped backward and out of her embrace. An uneasy burst of laughter followed. "You touch me now and there's no way I'll make it through the night."

"When?" She heard the need in her own voice. The scent of her arousal hung heavy in the air and thickened with thoughts of taking his cock into her mouth. She almost closed her eyes to savor what it would feel like to dip her tongue into the slit at the head of his erection and taste the salty come she knew would be there.

His eyes dilated as she shared her thoughts with him. "Stop that," he demanded, shifting his hips. "Woman, you're killing me." His hand rose as if to touch her, but it fell back to his side. "Later, after the crowd goes home." His voice was hoarse. "Then the morning is ours."

That was a promise Fallon fully expected him to deliver, because right now she was hurting with the need to touch him. She wanted to run her hands over all that solid muscle. Feel him tremble beneath her palms. This powerful man was hers, at least for the time she remained in Northern Arizona.

And then she would even the score with Chavez.

Chapter Seven

It was pushing midnight and the party raged on with no signs of breaking. When one fire burned low another log was added to breathe life into it again. An impressive dent had been made in the food, thanks to his guests. Several more barrels of beer had been tapped.

Good news was that everyone appeared to be enjoying themselves, even Fallon. Or was it a façade? He couldn't help noticing her watchful eye. The way a shadow would slither across her face as if she regretted enjoying herself.

"What do you know about her?" Briar asked. Adrian's friend stared long and hard at him, before he knelt close to the ground, running a stick through the dark soil.

His back to a tree, Adrian glanced toward Fallon. Her soft laughter rose above everyone else's to stroke his ears. She was sitting across from Maggie at a picnic table. Whatever she said forced a giggle from Maggie. It had been a long time since he had heard her laugh. Not that she had much to laugh about since she came to him.

"Not much," Adrian admitted. "Fallon's running from something or someone."

Sometimes Adrian felt his home was for wayward vampires. Crystal, the slender brunette who walked up beside Maggie, had been with him for about ten years. Doreen, the busty blonde who called

Crystal away to help refurbish the soda pop, had lived at his ranch for the last five years. And of course, Maggie had been with him for three years.

"That can't be good," Briar commented.

"Nah. I'm sure it isn't."

The stick in Briar's hand stopped in mid-stroke. "What went on this morning?"

"Bad dream," Adrian offered, but nothing more. There had been no time when they arose to question her and for some reason he felt it would have been a worthless attempt. Unless he probed her memories he wouldn't find anything out until she told him. His promise to leave her thoughts untouched was probably not a good decision.

He watched as Fallon slipped her hand across the table to rest upon Maggie's. Maggie retreated, pulling her hand into her lap. He couldn't miss the similarities between women. Neither trusted easily and both appeared to be running from shadows. Fallon's he hadn't discovered. Maggie had been attacked by a Master vampire. If Adrian ever got his hands on the demon, he would kill him.

"Maybe it'd be best to send her on her way."

Adrian jerked his head around pinning Briar with a glare.

Briar held his hands up, stick wedged between his fingers, palms facing Adrian. "All I'm saying, Boss, is this gal has turned your head. You're different around her."

Adrian's anger rose hot and fast. His chin slowly dropped as he looked through narrowed eyes. "Are you questioning my ability to lead?" The fine hairs on his neck stood on end. His fury energized the air around them. He didn't attempt to quiet his feelings, drawing several of his people's eyes, including Fallon's and Maggie's.

"Absolutely not," Briar said quickly, adjusting his hat, again. Yet he waited until everyone went back to their business before he continued. "Women mess with a man's head." A hollowness echoed in his voice as if he knew it to be true from personal experience.

Strange, because all the time Adrian had known Briar he had never spoken of a woman. The man kept to himself. It wasn't Adrian's place to meddle.

"I'll admit that Fallon intrigues me."

Briar huffed, a breathy sign of disbelief. "Intrigue? Heard that one before." He pulled his hat further down over his eyes, tossed the stick aside and rose. "She's got you fuckin' tied in knots." His friend nodded in an upward gesture. "That hard-on isn't because you're happy to see me." A low, deep chuckle rose, before he said, "All I'm saying is…be careful. A woman like her means trouble."

As if to emphasize the point two men approached Fallon and Maggie. They spoke, and then both women rose. A well-muscled man stepped to Fallon's side, while the tall lanky cowboy took Maggie by the hand. Fallon flashed her partner a brilliant smile as hand in hand they headed for the dance floor.

Adrian's immediate reaction was to lunge forward and rescue Fallon from the man who pulled her into his arms as the music started. Instead Briar's interested stare kept him rooted to the tree he leaned against.

It's just a dance.

Fallon moved in fluid motions, easing in and out of the man's embrace. Her hips had a sexy sway as she two-stepped to the beat of the music. It was as if the melody guided her from one step to the next. Her hair hung loosely. Then a gentle breeze whispering through the trees raised it from her shoulders and the dark curtain floated around the two dancing, in a sensual embrace. The cowboy buried his nose in her mane as he scented her soft perfume.

The tenderness in her face as she mouthed the words of the song had Adrian pushing away from the tree. His body tensed, wanting to feel her in his arms.

It's just a dance.

Bottom line she meant nothing to him. Like he had said earlier, she intrigued him. He watched the cowboy draw her closer so that their lips almost met.

A low growl rumbled in Adrian's throat. The heat of jealousy rose forcing him to take a step forward.

Who was he kidding? She did mean something to him. He had felt it the moment she hit town. The damn woman slithered right beneath his skin and refused to release the hold she had on him. Yet, there was no doubt in his mind, if he had to choose between his people and Fallon—Fallon would lose.

His duty was to his people.

Still that little nagging sensation pulled at him telling him to get Fallon out of the cowboy's arms and into his. Or better yet—into his bed.

As he left Briar behind and crossed the distance between him and Fallon, he thought of calling down the rain. But there wasn't a cloud in the sky. Of course he could make everyone think it was later than it was. Yet, that would be selfish. Everyone was having such a good time.

His guard went on full alert when he saw Maggie cast a shield around her and the cowboy she danced with. She leaned in and pierced the man's throat. To everyone on the dance floor it would just look like they were kissing. But he saw through the illusion, as well as many of his people.

A loud roar rose above the chatter and music. Then all hell broke loose.

Tucker appeared from out of nowhere, standing beside Maggie. He ripped the cowboy out of her arms sending the man crashing into people and landing with a thud as he tumbled off the dance floor into the grass.

Maggie released a high pitch scream of surprise. "Tucker! Oh my God."

As she made to run to the cowboy's side, Adrian felt Tucker's anger soar, felt the magic he hurled toward Maggie that paralyzed her feet. She attempted to move. With her own strength she tried to break the spell, but it was futile.

"Damn you, Tucker," she cried.

From across the yard, Adrian used magic to quickly close the wound at the cowboy's throat. Already the man's blood was seeping upon his shirt.

The crowd separated as the two men took each other's measure.

A fight always fired the masses and this had all the signs of something that could get way out of hand—and quickly. Voices rose and already he could hear betting amongst the crowd on which cowboy would win.

The human was no match for Tucker. And a pissed Tucker was even more dangerous.

From the rage burning in Tucker's eyes Adrian would have thought it was enough to keep the cowboy at bay. But no such luck. The man rose and crossed the distance between them. As the lanky cowboy balled his fist and swung, Adrian ensured the punch connected with Tucker's jaw, adding his own strength behind the man's.

Tucker's feet flew out from beneath him and he skidded across the dance floor on his ass. The shocked expression on Tucker's face, as well as all the vampires' in attendance couldn't be missed.

All eyes turned to Adrian. He simply cocked a brow of satisfaction.

Tucker had stepped out of line. Adrian couldn't allow one of his people to physically harm a human, especially over something as simple as feeding. Tucker himself had taken Donna's blood out on the dance floor during the last dance.

Before Tucker could rise, Adrian sent a mental command for Cougar and Briar to restrain the vamp. He fought them like a madman, but it was useless. All the time his hot gaze was riveted on Maggie.

With just a thought, Adrian disarmed Tucker's mental powers. Silently, he sent a couple of men to the human cowboy to make sure the fight ended now. He wanted the guy escorted to his truck and a guard sent with him, just in case Tucker decided to strike out at him later.

With Adrian's interference of Tucker's magic Maggie was able to break his spell. Silent tears fell as she took one last look at Tucker, then turned and fled.

Adrian didn't miss the simmering glare Tucker tossed him. His chest heaved. *"Adrian, release me."*

Cougar and Briar might have their hands on his biceps, but Tucker knew who controlled the situation.

Adrian nodded, releasing his mental hold on Tucker.

Tucker shrugged from Cougar and Briar's grips, and without delay broke into a run to chase after Maggie.

Adrian gave a silent order for the band to play.

From the corner of his eye he saw Fallon refuse to dance with the cowboy she stood by. He reached out to grab her. Before Adrian could do anything Fallon diffused the situation by simply disappearing. Not quite how Adrian would have approached it, but effective all the same. The man stood speechless, a look of confusion plastered on his face before he turned and strolled off the dance floor.

The light mist Fallon became was invisible to the human eye, but not his, as she drifted high above the throng, materializing by his side.

Adrian slipped his arm around her shoulders and pulled her close. She came willingly. But he wasn't through with Tucker.

"*Tucker.*" Adrian used the mind link between them to speak to his friend, as he simultaneously used his power to calm the crowd.

"*Yeah.*" Tucker's response was filled with remorse.

"*I don't have to remind you what Maggie has been through. Hurt her…you'll answer to me.*"

"*Shit, Adrian. You know I wouldn't hurt her.*" Adrian heard the truth in Tucker's voice, but his earlier actions hadn't been extremely convincing. "*Where did the damn woman go anyway?*" He heard Tucker's frustration. Adrian also knew that if Maggie didn't want to be found there was no way Tucker would find her.

"Well that was exciting," Fallon said, but the frown on her face said differently. "That blond Adonis needs his ass kicked." She bristled beneath his arm.

"There's a story there. Tucker cares very deeply for Maggie, as we all do." His admission deepened her scowl. He could imagine her mind working to figure out Maggie's and his relationship.

Intimacy—there was none.

No man had touched Maggie since she arrived in his town. That's why it was surprising that she had done what she had on the dance floor. Maggie only fed from women, and of course he had shared his blood with her to save her life those several years ago.

"Well that kind of caring a girl can do without." Fallon tensed. "In fact, a woman needs to learn how to protect herself."

He gave her a little squeeze. "Why when she has a man to do it for her?"

Fallon felt like decking Adrian. Her fingers curled into tight fists. "That was a chauvinistic reply." She tried to duck beneath his arm, but he maneuvered her so that her back was pinned against a tree.

So like a man.

He placed his hands on either side of her face and leaned into her. "It's been this way since the dawn of time." His amused grin only fired her frustration.

"Well. We're not in the dark ages anymore," she snapped. "Men are more a threat to women than—than breast cancer. More women die at the hands of a man than any disease or accident." Her heart thrummed in her chest. Could she lead him right toward the subject she so desperately needed to discuss? And so soon?

His lips moved against hers. "Darlin', I'll teach you anything you want to know."

She released the taut breath she held. "Yeah. Sure you would." Again, she tried to duck beneath his arms. Only to find herself drawn to his chest, locked in his arms.

Her heart was racing. Could she be so close to finally discovering Chavez's secrets?

"I mean it, Fallon. But I'd rather you let me fight your battles."

God, that sounded too good to be true, and of course it was. As in honor between thieves, she was sure there was some unwritten law between Master vampires. She knew they never tread on each other's property, and by all means Fallon was Chavez's property.

"Forget it." She feigned indifference. If she acted too excited, too interested, it would only spike his suspicion.

He looked at her and she could see it was too late. A shadow of doubt flickered in his eyes. "What is it you want to learn?" he asked hesitantly.

"Hell, I don't know—" She softened her expression and voice. She attempted to reflect guiltless eyes as she looked up at him. "Well, for example what would happen if I came across a Master vampire, like you for instance, and needed to protect myself?"

Boy, did that sound sappy. She couldn't hope that he would buy into the helpless woman scheme.

Fallon held her breath, waited for the moment he would tell her to pack her bags and leave. Been there—done that. This was always the point where she found herself moving on or even threatened.

Seconds felt like minutes as he gazed into her eyes. "I'd never hurt you."

Where did that come from? She placed a palm against his chest. "Oddly, I know that. Still, I can hold my own with many vampires—male or female." She glanced away as she lied. "Maybe that isn't even true after what I saw Tucker do to Maggie. But what about a stronger—older vampire—a Master? How would someone like me defend myself?" Okay, the poor, innocent woman card was cheesy, but it was the only one she had left.

With a single finger he raised her chin so that their eyes met. "Fallon, are you in some kind of trouble?"

She tried to brush off his question with laughter that died too soon to be convincing even to her. "No. Just concerned. Since I travel alone

I want to be prepared for anything or anyone. I've only been wearing the immortal shoes for a year and a half." Her pitiful excuses were failing miserably if the deep set wrinkles in his forehead were any sign. Thank goodness he didn't try to touch her mind.

"You know as a vampire we live an awful long time," she added.

His hands slipped to her biceps. "Maybe you should tell me what's going on." He looked at her with such compassion that guilt rode her hard.

Darn if lying to him wasn't becoming more difficult. For some strange reason she felt as if he knew she was deceiving him. Her stomach twisted.

What was she thinking? This was never going to work. "Never mind. I'll find out what I need from someone else." At least that was the truth.

What made her think she could waltz into his world and that he would spill his guts? Willingly arm her with knowledge that could place him as well as his people in danger.

What a fool she was. Stupid. Stupid. Stupid.

It was time to move on. If she left now she could probably be in Phoenix or Yuma before the sun rose. Maybe she'd head to California. She'd never been to California.

Fallon tipped her chin, perched on her toes, and pressed her lips to his. A moment of sorrow hit her hard as her heels slowly touched the ground. She trembled with the feeling of emptiness that seeped deep into her bones. With as much bravado as she could muster she forced the emotion back. "It's time for me to go."

"Go?" Confusion pulled his brows together.

"Down the road. Adios. Ciao." Fallon forced a smile that received a frown from him. She patted him again on the chest. "Don't want to overstay my welcome. Besides the road is calling me." She shrugged indifferently. "Guess I'm a gypsy at heart."

That was such a lie. She hated running. All her life all she wanted was roots, a family to call her own, and to be loved. For the briefest of moments she had glimpsed that with Christy. Then everything changed. All she wanted now was revenge and to join her daughter.

"You're kidding, right?" he asked as his palms slid from her arms.

"Nope. It's time." Better to leave now, than for him to toss her out when he discovered her real reason for wanting to be with him.

God, she was really going to miss him. He was one mighty fine kisser.

No. It had to be their blood connection. That was the only thing that made sense.

Fallon turned to leave, but the next thing she knew she was spun around and wrapped in his arms. Before she could resist he quieted her with his mouth. The kiss was firm, his tongue invading, demanding her surrender.

And like an idiot—she surrendered—giving as well as taking what he offered, sending her body into flames. She clutched her hands into his shirt. Pressed her hips closer to his, needing to feel his heat—his strength. Breasts heavy, her nipples tingled, aching for his touch. Already she was damp with desire.

But much too soon it was over, leaving her breathless, aroused, and facing Adrian's dark, questioning eyes.

"Darlin', you're not going anywhere." His arms tightened around her as if to prove his words. "Not before we talk."

"Not now, Adrian." Words she didn't want. She rubbed her body against the firm bulge in his jeans. "Fuck me instead. We'll talk later."

Chapter Eight

The band played the last chord, a beautiful blend of steel guitar, bass and fiddle, before announcing that the next song would be the final one of the night. The moans of disappointment were only murmurs to Adrian as he held Fallon close. Soon everyone would be leaving, but she wouldn't be one of them. Not if he had anything to say about it—and he did.

The cool breeze that brushed his face was a completely different sensation against his heightened skin to that of Fallon's warm body pressed to his. The scent of her arousal, hot and sensual, only fed his need to strip her naked and fuck her hard and fast. Not to mention the way she rubbed against his already throbbing cock was driving him out of his mind. Even the need to discover why she wanted to leave was quickly taking second place to his desire to bury himself deep inside her warmth.

Was it a diversion? A way to change the subject?

It didn't matter—it was working.

With a quick brush of his arm beneath the bend of her knees, he cradled her to his chest. The soft, sexy smile she gifted him with as she weaved her arms around his neck put his feet in motion. As she snuggled close, teasing the vein that pulsed in his neck with her tongue, he thought of just dropping to the ground, taking her here—now.

"Boss—"

"Not now, Cougar." Adrian hastened his steps, fully aware that his friend followed. Damn, the man.

"But—"

"Not now Cougar," Adrian grumbled. This couldn't be happening. What was so important that it couldn't wait? Short of the house being on fire he was going to make love to Fallon.

"We can't find Maggie."

Cougar's words jerked Adrian to a stop. Fallon's head rose, so that they were eye to eye. Gently, he released her until her feet settled on the ground. He pivoted to face Cougar. "How long has she been missing?"

"Since the fight." Cougar grew eerily silent, tucking his fingers into his jean pockets. His sullen expression only added to the anxiety growing beneath Adrian's skin, which had started to prickle, tiny sharp needles raising the hair on his arms. Even Fallon's soft hand on his chest didn't repel the sense of apprehension building inside him.

He hated to ask, but did anyway. "And?"

"And Tucker is beside himself." Cougar shook his head, sending his long, black braid swaying side to side. "The man's going crazy trying to find her."

"Shit." Adrian inhaled and released the air slowly from his lungs as he opened his links to both Maggie and Tucker.

The mass of chaos that erupted in Adrian's mind was from Tucker. In the form of a large eagle he soared above the ground releasing a mournful screech that echoed in Adrian's head. Feelings of desperation, anger and fear rang clear in the next harsh shriek that stung his ears.

But there was nothing from Maggie. Absolutely nothing. She wasn't even a blip on his radar screen, which in itself meant trouble. Either she had traveled beyond his ability to track her or someone was blocking his signal. There hadn't been enough time for her to get very far. And he truly didn't want to think about the only other alternative.

"Adrian?" Fallon reached out to touch his mind, but he closed their connection before she could hear his thoughts. She didn't need to know the horrors Maggie had experienced.

When Maggie arrived just outside the White Mountain Apache Reservation three years ago she had been close to death, nearly drained of blood. A ravished, frightened creature, she had been too weak to resist his help. All compliments of her Master. A man Adrian had never met, but looked forward to meeting every time he touched Maggie's mind and found her scared and questioning why he saved her life. Death had been better than the fear she lived with every day wondering when her Master would find her.

Another deep breath and he mentally reached for the land to see if any traces of disturbance existed. Again he found nothing. Then the slightest of ripples stirred him. It was all he needed. He knew where Maggie was.

"Fallon, go to ground," he barked his command, ignoring her as he turned inwardly to warn his people and call for assistance. As multiple voices rang in his head, the one beside him was the loudest.

"I want to help." Fallon's voice was filled with concern.

"I can't be worried about you." His response was curt, too abrupt. The result showed across her face as her features tightened. But he didn't have time to apologize.

Without another word his bones began to pop—shifting. Like always the pain came and vanished, quickly replaced by a flood of tingles across his skin as a light down of feathers sprung from his pores. Wings formed where once his arms had been. His legs and feet morphed into strong talons. He raised his beak toward the sky and released a cry of his own.

And then he was airborne.

It hurt to be dismissed. Even more to be considered a burden.

Well hell. What did Fallon expect?

This was the opportunity she was looking for. With Adrian preoccupied she could slip from town and he wouldn't be any the wiser. Yet, leaving at this particular moment just didn't feel right.

Maggie was in trouble.

Dammit. She had her own troubles to think about. Still she couldn't help sensing that Maggie and she had a lot in common. Both saw shadows where shadows weren't cast. Trust was an issue. Even as they spoke together, Fallon could feel Maggie probing her. At first Fallon had thought it was because she was new to the area. But deeper into the conversation she sensed there was more, as if every stranger held a potential for danger.

Fallon knew what that felt like.

While Fallon physically ran from her problems, traveling from one place to another, Maggie ran within her mind, like a caged animal.

They were two of a kind.

Before Fallon realized it she dissolved into mist. She had never been able to take form so easily. When she made the transformation on the dance floor she contributed the ease to Adrian's blood exchanges. Where normally she felt heavy and worked to keep afloat tonight she felt light and airy. Buoyantly, she moved through the trees, fast and silent, using her link to Adrian to lead her.

This time when a gust of air whipped through her misty form she didn't struggle to maintain a steady stream of moisture. Instead she used the breeze to her favor, actually willing the current to turn so that it assisted her instead of impeded her progression.

Then a disturbance in the sky shook her—she began to drop. For a second, the sharp fall rattled her confidence. She quickly gathered her composure, but not without noticing that the elements around her were crying out in pain. It was in the moan of the wind, the trembling of the trees as the earth shook.

Something evil had arrived.

For a moment she couldn't breathe. The tranquility of the night had vanished.

Dark, gray clouds choked out the moon and stars that had once brightened the heavens. Below her the stream that previously flowed at a gentle current splashed angrily against its confines. White caps formed as it crashed into rocks and fallen logs. Even nature resisted as she heard the roar of a bear, the lone cry of a wolf, and the fluttering of wings as a flock of turkeys exploded from the bushes heading in the opposite direction.

It should have been Fallon's warning to turn back, but she focused on the steady beat of Adrian's heart.

Then a strangled scream rented the air. The high-pitch, breathy cry filled with pain.

Maggie.

Fallon had no idea what to expect as she materialized. She stood amongst the trees out of sight. Three vampires she had never seen before stood over Maggie's bloody and crumpled form lying on the tall grass. She didn't move. Fallon couldn't see if she was breathing.

"The bitch is none of your concern," the man in the middle growled. Brown shoulder-length hair feathered back from his face with the strong breeze. His features were hardened and drawn. But the aura around him emanated power.

Fallon knew she was in the presence of a Master vampire. All were dressed in black pants and shirts, but where their leader was refined, the other two men on each side of him looked somewhat unkempt, disheveled. Their dark brunette hair was tangled and uncombed. Their clothes were skewed and wrinkled as if they slept in them. It showed a lack of character, which probably went along with the company they kept.

A loud menacing howl tore from Tucker's throat as he lunged, stopping mid-air when Briar and Cougar grabbed his arms. "Let me go." His breaths had turned into snarls and grunts, animalistic sounds that sent a chill up Fallon's spine.

The two vampires beside the Master vampire started toward Tucker, but halted when the Master said, "He's mine." He raised a hand before him, palm skyward. With a curl of his fingers, he taunted Tucker to come get him.

Tucker lunged again, but fell back against the two men restraining him. "You sonofabitch!" His gaze fell upon Maggie and his struggles to be released started again.

From behind an outcrop of rocks appeared Adrian. The beauty of the man made Fallon's heart stop. Each step he took was that of a predator, silent and lethal. The relaxed muscles in his face gave the impression of unleashed power held lightly under control. If he was frightened or concerned about the outcome of this meeting, his composure didn't reveal it.

"*Ahhh*...Dominic. So nice of you to visit." Not once did he gaze down at Maggie. Instead he kept his eyes on the Master. Still Fallon felt his mind quickly assess Maggie, feeding back the information to his people.

"She's badly hurt." Tucker cried out using their mental link.

"When the situation is under control take her back to the house. Immediately, start transfusions. Fallon, you will return with the others."

Crap. Crap. Crap. Adrian knew she was here. And by the grumble in his voice he wasn't happy.

"Damn straight I'm mad, young lady. But I'll deal with you later."

Okay, this wasn't good.

The grin that surfaced on Adrian's face was jovial as he met Dominic's gaze. "I see your manners haven't improved. Still picking on women." He made a clucking sound with his tongue. "Not very gentlemanly." The smile faded from his face. In its place appeared a loathsome expression that made even Fallon take a step backward. "You dare to come upon my land without requesting permission." His voice deepened with authority.

Dominic hauled back his foot and swung forward, catching Maggie in the ribs. "This is my permission." Her soft, tortured cry brought another roar from Tucker.

For the first time since Fallon arrived she felt anger rise in Adrian. As if it were alive, it seeped from his pores into the air charging it with his power. Raw. Omnipotent strength that burned, singeing whatever particulars in the air that dared to draw near him.

In a low, rough timbre, he promised, "You'll never hurt her again."

With preternatural speed, Adrian attacked. His ghostly image soared through the air, striking Dominic and his two men and slinging them back away from Maggie. Like a savior dressed in Wranglers, boots, and a Stetson he stood over the broken woman.

Roots sprung up from the ground around Dominic's minions, wrapping and trapping the lesser vampires. The two men shrieked and fought, but to no avail as more thick shoots rose and slithered across the surface. The Master vampire pulled through them like they were butter. When he discovered he couldn't release his men from Adrian's spell Dominic shook with fury. He raised mid-air and glared down upon Adrian.

"You have broken the law. She is mine to do with as I wish. And I wish her dead." Dominic thrust his hand out, sending a sharp, broken limb from the ground into the air and hurled it toward Maggie's limp body. Before the makeshift stake touched her it burst into pieces, the small kindling sprinkling over her like sawdust.

"*Move her,*" Adrian demanded as he put himself between Maggie and Dominic. Briar and Cougar released Tucker and he fled to Maggie's side.

"Honey." Tucker's voice shook as he knelt.

Dominic roared as his feet touched the ground. Fallon covered her ears. The sound was so loud it vibrated her eardrums. The lesser vampires were slowly breaking through the myriad of roots binding them.

"*Now!*" The urgency in Adrian's mental voice brought Cougar and Briar to Tucker's side as he raised her in his arms. Fallon felt Maggie's weakness. She'd never be able to shape-shift.

Power radiated off Adrian. In disbelief, Fallon watch Maggie's body melt into Tucker's to form one. He raised his head, a gasp escaping his parted mouth as he rose to his feet. With a soft expression he placed a hand over his heart, and then took the form of an eagle. Cougar made the change and, as two large birds, they rose into the sky. Although they were massive, the human world would see somewhat normal size birds as they flew through the sky.

Fallon was still gazing skyward at the show of strength in Adrian's magic when he rumbled, "*Fallon.*"

Shit! What a quandary. Obey Adrian or stay and experience exactly what she needed to learn—how to destroy a Master vampire.

When Adrian released a low note of disapproval she wasn't sure whether it was for her disobedience or the upcoming battle. Fact was that wild horses couldn't drag her away from this spot.

Briar sidled up to Adrian. The two men looked dangerous side by side—like avenging angels.

Adrian's voice was eerily calm when he said, "Now it's time for us to dance."

Energy filled the night air like nothing Fallon had ever experienced. It actually raised the soft down across her body. From out of nowhere the wind became violent whirling masses that whipped her hair back and forth. She had to restrain it with her hands as she fought to keep it out of her face so that she could observe.

From the clouds above Adrian and Briar, golf-ball size hail shot from the sky, a sheet of white falling at blinding speed. Before the deadly pieces of ice struck they exploded into flurries of powdery snow that fell heavily upon the two men to create a blanket of white at their feet.

In unison, both Adrian and Briar brushed the crystalline flakes off their shoulders like they were bothersome at best. Snow lay in the rims of their Stetsons. It would have been funny if the situation weren't so volatile.

"You can do better than that, Dominic," Adrian taunted.

Dominic's laugh was sinister. "I have no plans to kill you slowly. But when I do your people are mine."

Fallon noticed that the two vampires who had been caught in roots and vines had broken free. They were a blur as they moved toward Adrian and Briar disappearing in thin air only to reappear behind them.

"Cocky son of a bitch, isn't he?" Briar chuckled, but there was no amusement in his tone.

A tick raised the corner of Adrian's mouth into a snarl baring his fangs. "You can try."

Both vampires snickered. Fallon felt their confidence as they trapped Adrian and Briar between them and their Master. But neither Adrian nor Briar appeared affected by this fact.

Fallon didn't know how they could remain calm. She was shaking so badly her teeth chattered.

Then everything happened fast.

When the three vampires began to close in, Adrian's and Briar's reach was deadly and accurate.

Their fingertips became razor sharp talons, arcing into wicked weapons. In unison, they somersaulted high above the lesser vampires. Their hands shimmered against the dark as they sliced through the air and their enemies.

The horrific screams of Dominic's two minions as their life essence squirted from their throats and wrists sent shivers down Fallon's spine.

Their eyes bulged.

Their mouths were agape.

Desperately, their hands grasped their throats attempting to stop the flow of blood and life.

At the same time Dominic disappeared, avoiding any contact and reappearing at a safe distance. With a swipe of his hand, he commanded several large trees to fall right atop both Adrian and Briar.

Fallon's heart stuttered. Still she didn't hesitate invoking her magic to slow the progression of the heavy trees. That small act of courage won her two things. One, the attention of Dominic, and two, a disapproving growl from Adrian as he and Briar stepped aside out of danger.

The trees crashed with a forceful thud, shaking the ground beneath her.

What happened next between Briar and the lesser vampires, she didn't know. Fallon was more concerned with the two powerful men who had her in their scope. Both with an expression that said they would like to kill her.

She attempted to shape-shift, only managing to lightly shimmer. She could feel the strong push and pull of both Dominic's and Adrian's power targeted at her. Fear raced across her skin as nausea twisted in her stomach.

"Come to me, little one." Dominic's enticement was a dark weave of evil. It burned across her skin like acid.

Adrian remained quiet. His expression was intense and focused, until he pivoted and lunged at Dominic.

Claws and fangs were all she saw through a cloud of black that surrounded the two like a shroud.

Growls and hisses sounded. Grunts and moans followed.

She struggled to see past the dark veil with no luck. But she felt unleashed power vibrate through the earth and up her legs. When she felt a cold, ruthless feeling of triumph rise, she held her breath afraid to watch any further—afraid not to.

What if Adrian failed to defeat Dominic?

A bloodcurdling scream sent tears down her cheeks.

When the cloud thinned Adrian stood above the fallen Master. Both were bloodied, large tears to their clothing. Fallon didn't want to even think what had been done to their bodies. Dominic slithered upon the ground like a wounded animal toward Adrian.

"You haven't won." Dominic's voice was a hoarse gurgle as he held tight to his defiance.

Adrian stepped out of the way. Again an intense expression hardened his face. Fallon felt his power combine with Briar's, who moved beside him. Together their magic crashed into Dominic's body, which began to thrash and then exploded like a stick of dynamic was triggered inside him.

Fallon jerked her sight away, closing her eyes. When she finally opened them again neither Dominic nor his minions were anywhere in sight. What remained was destruction of the land. She wanted to cry at the beauty that was gone. In its place—scorched and blackened trees and ground. The depraved scent of Dominic's evilness remained, mingling with the scent of burning pine.

A light rain began to fall. Drops landed on her eyelashes causing her to blink, before she glanced at Adrian. A deep, heavy rolling sound rose deep from his chest.

"Okay. Okay. I'm going," she said frantically. Without a second thought she imaged a light mist and shape-shifted. Before Fallon got out of earshot she heard Briar say, "Now she obeys you."

Chapter Nine

Back at Adrian's house, Fallon watched Tucker cradle Maggie's sleeping form in his arms as he sat in a rocking chair by her bed. Slowly he swayed back and forth. A gentle creak sounded each time he moved forward. As he tucked the blanket around her shoulders, he dipped his head and mumbled something close to her ear, too softly for Fallon to hear.

"Would you like for me to feed her?" Fallon asked.

Tucker's head rose sharply. "No! I mean I've given her two transfusions already."

"Can I supply you with substance?" she offered freely.

He shook his head. "I fed from Crystal and Doreen earlier."

Fallon remembered the two vampires. Crystal was a statuesque brunette who always seemed to have her eyes pinned on Adrian. Doreen was a full-figured blonde who appeared a little offish, but only toward Fallon. To everyone else, especially Susan's children, the woman was kind and loving.

It hurt when Tucker shunned her help, but she did understand. Since no one knew who she was or where she came from, her blood was too risky. Besides she wouldn't wish any of them to have ties to Pedro Chavez. Just the thought of him made Fallon wrap her arms around herself. She trembled, feeling a chill slide across her skin.

Maggie and she had a lot in common. Both were hunted by the devils themselves.

Adrian had ridded Maggie of her tormenter this evening. The woman was physically safe, but Fallon knew what mental war would rage on in Maggie's mind for some time—maybe forever.

Fallon looked up at the clock that flashed 2:00 am. Her stomach churned, knot after knot developing with each minute that ticked by.

Where was Adrian?

He was so angry with her. Did she dare wait to bear his fury or should she run like a coward? The thought of never seeing him again almost brought tears to her eyes. She felt them hot against her eyelids.

And what had she learned tonight that would help her in her pursuit to conquer Chavez? First she had to bleed him, and then kill him from the inside out. How was she going to do that?

"Is there anything I can do?" she asked Tucker, moving closer to him.

The raw pain in his eyes as he looked up at Fallon squeezed her chest. Silently he just shook his head. Then he dropped his gaze back to Maggie.

Dark rings shadowed her swollen eyes. There was a gash above one brow that was already beginning to mend. Bruises and other cuts appeared on her face. Fallon shuddered at the thought of what other damage Dominic had ravaged on Maggie's poor body…and mind.

There were just some things a woman would never forget. She tried to push the thought away, burying these reminders with all the ones deep in her subconscious.

What baffled Fallon now was Tucker's attention toward Maggie. If Fallon hadn't seen Tucker with other women, she would have said he loved Maggie. But that just didn't make sense.

Males. It didn't matter what species, if she lived forever she didn't think she'd ever understand them.

When the door creaked open and Adrian stepped inside, Fallon forced herself not to run to him. He was freshly dressed in a clean pair of blue jeans and a plaid western shirt of different shades of tans and browns. His boots looked like they had been buffed and he wore a different cowboy hat. The light scent of aftershave tickled her nose.

It hurt that he ignored her and strolled straight to Maggie. But she probably should consider herself lucky.

"I'll feed her." Adrian's voice sounded terse.

"I've seen to her needs," Tucker snarled.

"My blood will heal her quicker," Adrian stated.

Tucker's response was a low warning deep in his throat, as he tightened his grasp on Maggie.

"Be careful, Tucker." Caution spoke loudly in Adrian's words. "She is precious to us all, and you have tested my limits this day."

Without a second thought, Adrian tore open his wrist and pressed it to Maggie's swollen lips. Her mouth moved, but she was too weak to drink. Fallon knew when Adrian used his own strength to help her feed. Immediately, Maggie's fangs sank into Adrian's wrist. When she was finished Adrian extracted his arm, closing the wound himself.

Then Adrian turned to face Fallon. His expression was unreadable. "You." Her eyes widened. "Come with me." It was all he said before he headed to the door, not checking to see if she followed.

But she did. And she had no doubt she was in big trouble.

Adrian was on the brink of losing control. Not only had he been tested by a Master this day, but Tucker, not to mention Fallon, had disobeyed him. His footsteps were loud on the wooden floor as he walked down the hallway to his bedroom. In the process, he stormed by Sally and Gary, who had the good sense not to speak to him, nor did Briar as he backed into the shadows of an alcove.

Tucker he would deal with later. For what remained of the night he would address Fallon's disregard of his authority.

He swung open the door and gazed into the fireplace that had a small fire glowing inside its grate. Fallon's featherlight steps sounded in the room behind him.

"Close the door." The hinges creaked as she followed his directions.

"Adrian?" Her voice was soft, hesitant.

Without turning around, he said. "Take your clothes off." He was so fucking hard from battle lust that he didn't know if he could wait long enough to punish Fallon, before driving his cock deep inside her. Just the thought made his balls tighten painfully.

"What?" Surprise raised her voice.

Moving was difficult, but he turned and faced her, letting the heat he felt fill the room. Wide-eyed, she began to toe off one of her boots. She stumbled, almost fell, but managed to remove both boots and socks.

As she fumbled with the buckle of her belt, she said, "I'm sorry. I just—"

"The pants and shirt." Damn. She was beautiful, but he wasn't going to allow that to deter him. She had blatantly disobeyed. When Dominic had sighted her, Adrian literally died a little inside.

"But—"

"*Now…*" He heard her pulse speed, the sweet sound of her blood swishing through her veins. Knew the moment she realized that he was truly unhappy with her, because she trembled.

Then she stilled, straightened her body to full height as she drew her shoulders back with a jerk. "Wait just one minute," she grumbled, a frown marring her pretty features. "I'm not accustomed to obeying anyone. Besides I saved your ass from those trees. Shouldn't you be thanking me?"

"Darlin', you are one nervy broad." He took slow, measured steps toward her, keeping her sight trapped in his. "I call the shots in my town. And you will obey me." Man, he wanted to feel her beneath him as he pumped in and out of her hot, wet pussy.

She huffed. "In your dreams—"

A tight squeal left her mouth as the remainder of her clothing disappeared with his command.

Mouth parted, she scanned her naked body, before tossing him a heated glare. "Give me back my clothes."

He ignored her and instead, he said, "Get on your hands and knees before the fire."

Her eyes became as big as saucers. "Adrian?" Her voice cracked.

He gave a firm nod toward the Persian rug lying before the fireplace. The flames in the hearth sprang to life, crackling and hissing.

With another huff of attitude she placed her fists on her hips. The look she gave him said "make me".

With blurring speed, he grabbed her arms and jerked her to his chest. He heard her breath release in surprise. Fully clothed, he could still feel the pebbling of her nipples. The fire in her eyes matched his own as he crushed his mouth to hers. Tense beneath his touch, she fought to keep her lips pressed tightly together, but it was useless. When he cupped her ass, wedging a finger in between the crevice of her cheeks, she gasped. Immediately, he took advantage and thrust his tongue into her mouth.

Surrender was not a choice—she was his. Before the night was over she would damn well know who she belonged to. Fallon would also learn to never disobey him.

Spirited. She attempted to pull away, to shun his kiss. But he held her firmly with a hand at the nape of her neck. A slant of his head, he deepened the kiss leaving nowhere in her mouth untouched.

He knew the moment he'd won. Her arms, which had been pressed to her sides, rose and slipped around his neck. But her kiss wasn't gentle as her tongue dueled with his. Teeth impacted with a clink. The pressure between their mouths increased and he tasted blood. His? Hers? It didn't matter, it fueled the flame beneath them both.

The low, broken sounds of her whimpers only raised his hunger. He growled in return, spearing his fingers through her hair pulling her head back to break the kiss.

Her chest rose and fell rapidly. Breathing labored, her eyes were bright with a blend of anger and desire. She was magnificent in her fury.

"Let me go," she snapped.

"Never." And he meant it. Sometime between when he walked in this room and he pressed his body to hers, he had come to the conclusion that Fallon was never walking out of his life—no matter what he had to do to keep her.

She pulled her arms from around his neck and tried to pry them between their bodies. "Adrian." His name came out a warning.

He tightened his grip on her hair and her eyes widened further. "Let me tell you how this night will play out. First, I'm going to tan your hide for disobeying me."

"You wouldn't dare?" Her disbelief came out in a breathy stream of air.

He raised a single brow and narrowed his gaze. "Next, I'm going to fuck you, darlin', so you don't ever think about leaving me." Her tongue made a nervous swipe between her swollen lips, drawing his attention. He mentally shook away the idea of skipping the spanking and going straight to the fucking. "Tomorrow morning you *will* tell me what is spooking you. And I *will not* take no for an answer."

With quick side-to-side movements, she shook her head. Her body trembled from head to toe as the fight inside her suddenly died. Breathing elevated, lips parted, she sucked in short gasps one after the other. For a moment he was afraid she would hyperventilate.

"Whatever it is we'll deal with it together." His voice softened to reassure her.

"Adrian." The hopelessness in her voice was hard to miss as was the fear in her eyes.

"Shhh…" He pulled her against him and held her until the trembling went away. When she started to relax she released a heavy sigh.

Hand in hand, he led her to the bed. It moaned beneath his weight as he sat. When he pulled her across his lap she cried, "Hey, wait—" She squirmed, fought like a wildcat to escape his hold. "I thought—"

"—that I'd forgotten your punishment. *Wrong…*" he hummed. Swiftly, he threw his right leg over her thighs, pinning her. His left hand pressed against her upper back to keep her stationary.

Her uneasy chuckle was muffled with her diaphragm pressed tight against his legs. "Uh—what about we forget the spanking and go straight to the fucking?"

"No can do." Adrian gently laid his palm on her bare ass and she flinched. He would have laughed, but the situation was serious. He felt her reach for her magic, but he froze it, disabling her from using it. "Fallon, you have no idea how the scene by the creek could have gotten out of control. Lives were in danger." Just the thought of losing Maggie—losing Fallon—made him intent on teaching her a lesson.

"I get it—I get it." The swiftness in her words was followed by, "Do you have to do this? Dammit. Adrian." Desperation rang in her voice. "This is humiliating. Why not a slap on the wrist? I promise to never disobey you again."

"And I promise after tonight you never *will* forget." The whack of his hand landing against her tender skin was loud. Even louder was Fallon's howl followed by, "You. Son. Of. A. Bitch," which only earned her another spanking.

Fuck. This was making him hot.

Just to see his mark rise pink and angry against her flesh made his cock harden painfully beneath Fallon's naked body. A body that he couldn't wait to stroke and make love to until dawn drove them to ground. He couldn't resist running his fingers between her thighs. The wetness he felt surprised him. Was this little temptress the slightest bit aroused by his spankings?

Whack!

Fallon arched her back and released a moan.

This time when he caressed her pussy a new flood of moisture anointed his fingers as he separated her swollen folds and slipped inside. God, she was wet. And hot. And tight. Slowly, he began to finger-fuck her, in and out, easy and deep.

"Adrian," she groaned.

He knew what she wanted. But she hadn't earned the right. Again, his hand met her ass, hard.

"*Adrian.*" This time his name was a cry upon her lips.

He couldn't help himself. His fingers found her slit again, and he entered her. She writhed beneath his touch, until he withdrew and slapped her ass, again. A firmly placed finger against her clit and she exploded.

"Yes," Fallon hissed as her hips rode his hand. He was relentless, moving his hand across her sensitive flesh, wringing every bit of sensation he could from her.

Ohhh…yeah. That was good.

The tingle between her thighs was oh-so-sweet. She felt like purring. And who knew that a spanking could entice such an exquisite climax? Or maybe it was the man delivering the punishment.

Pressed against her belly, Adrian's rock-hard cock told her just how much he had enjoyed this little scene. His breathing was harsh, but his hand gentle, soothing across her heated skin.

She inwardly laughed at his means of punishment that had backfired and turned into mind-blowing pleasure… That is until the feeling came back. As the height of her orgasm subsided and she started to relax, she noticed the burn that began to race across her ass.

Ow-ow-owie!

"Shit!" she screamed and attempted to move, but the pain increased leaving her breathless. "Fuck." The word came out on an exhale.

Adrian moved his leg releasing her. "On your hands and knees before the fire."

Lying across his lap, she turned her head so that she could see his face. "You're kidding, right?"

He shook his head. His expression hadn't changed since they came into his bedroom. That unreadable look about him was etched on his face. Was he still mad? Tentatively, she reached out mentally to determine his state of mind.

Bam! She hit what felt like a brick wall. For a moment she was dazed. The damn man wasn't sharing anything.

From where she stood or lay, she had two choices. One, do what he asked of her and see what the outcome would be. Or two, perhaps push him into punishing her again and by God her ass was burning. When she got her magic back this little episode would only be a memory.

Carefully, she pushed off his lap. The ache and sting in her ass as she rose was a reminder. When Adrian gave an order, he fully expected it to be carried through. Every footfall brought a silent cry to her lips and the desire to bitch-slap the man who stood and quietly began to undress.

Asshole.

"I heard that." A little of the gruffness from his voice had lifted and she could hear a hint of laughter seeping in.

Crap.

A gasp wedged in her throat as she caught sight of the angry red scars covering Adrian's gorgeous body. It appeared he had been badly whipped all over. The gaping slashes she knew had to exist were now puckered and swollen wounds already beginning to heal from his earlier battle with Dominic and his minions. She knew tomorrow night he would be good as new, as would she from Adrian's spanking. Still, her heart ached for him.

When she stood before the fire, the soft Persian rug beneath her feet, she began to sink to her knees. A new rush of scalding sensation burned across her ass as the tight skin was stretched tighter.

Damn. Damn. Damn. She prayed for the sun to rise and this night to be over.

"Hands and knees," he reminded her.

She leaned forward and her palms sank into the plush carpet. Fallon had no doubt that the submissive position was meant to be another form of punishment. From where he stood, she knew he could see her swollen folds. And for some crazy reason that turned her on.

The man had just delivered a hurtin' to her ass. It burned like a holy sonofabitch. And yet she couldn't stop thinking about how much she wanted him to take her from behind. Sink his rigid, thick cock deep inside her now moist pussy.

"Darlin', has anyone every told you what a mighty fine ass you have?" His sultry voice sent goose bumps up her arms.

Her belly did a flip-flop. Heat radiated off him as he grew closer. His hand touched her thigh as he knelt behind her.

"So nice and red—" he placed his palm on her ass, "—and hot."

She wanted to say "No fuck, Sherlock" but remained quiet, waiting for his next move. Fact was when he touched her, some of the pain in her butt had receded. Instead, she focused on his hands and what he was doing.

Tenderly he stroked from her knee to her thighs, over her abdomen, until he held her breasts in his palms. He pinched the peaks and the most delightful rays of sensations shot through her nipples.

"Pretty titties, too." Admiration softened his tone as he fondled and squeezed her globes. She felt the light kiss he placed on one ass cheek, and then his wet tongue licked a cooling path. When he blew on her moist skin a shiver raced up her spine.

Fallon had to admit that not being able to see him, his seductive voice coming from behind, and never knowing where his hands would caress next was beyond exciting. When he moved closer, his thighs to the back of hers and his cock nudged her slit, "Yes," slipped from her lips.

"Do you want me to fuck you?"

"Yes." There wasn't any use to pretend otherwise. She wanted him to ease the throb between her legs.

His hands left her breasts. For a heartbeat she waited for him to touch her again. When he did, she knew he held his own erection in his hand as his hardness slid across her labia, parting them briefly to increase the sensation. Just the thought of him grasping himself was heady. A moan vibrated in her throat. She moved her hips back, needing him to enter her. Instead he continued to tease, playing at her folds.

"Please, Adrian," she whimpered as her canines dropped, the taste of blood on her tongue. With each swipe across her tender skin the coil low in her belly wound tighter and tighter, pushing her higher and higher. She needed to touch him, to drive her fangs deep in his neck and taste his essences as he took her to heaven.

Positioned at her entrance, Adrian gripped her hips and then drove home, filling her with every inch of his cock.

Fallon closed her eyes, savoring the fullness. Buried deep inside he didn't move, as if he too needed a moment to enjoy the feeling of their bodies joined together. Then he began to rock, sliding in and out, slowly.

"Lean forward." His voice sounded strained. "Take all of me."

At first she didn't understand. And then she dropped down on her forearms, resting her head on her hands, ass up in the air, spreading her even wider.

He moved deeper inside her, filling her completely.

"Ahhh…fuck." He sucked in a ragged breath. "Yeah," he said on a breathy exhale and ground his hips, hitting a spot that threw Fallon over the precipice.

At the same time, Adrian's fingers dug into her ass sending needle-sharp pain through her skin. Her ass was so very sensitive. The pleasure/pain combination was so intense that her climax roared through her body, shaking her. One after another white-hot rays of sensation crashed through her body. She felt like a pin-ball machine. Her insides lighting up and sounds going off as the beams bounced off of one place to another.

A sudden thrust from behind almost made her collapse as Adrian joined her. A heavy groan from deep within his throat flowed past her ears, as his weight took her flat to the floor.

"Damn, woman," he murmured, pinning her beneath him. The rapid beat of his heart against her back pounded so loudly it echoed in her head.

In all her life, Fallon had never experienced such mind-blowing sex. Her body still hummed with aftershocks. Her nerves were raw. And she had worked up quite an appetite to taste Adrian. Her stomach growled.

"Your hunger is calling to me." He rose, withdrawing from her body and lifting his weight from hers.

Fallon couldn't quite manage to move, lying face down on the Persian rug. The heat of the fire was something she didn't need soaking into her already red-hot ass. She lacked the energy to rise. She smiled at her state of being, not remembering when she had ever felt so sated.

Strong but gentle hands slipped beneath her arms as Adrian assisted Fallon to her feet. He pulled her into his embrace and kissed her softly. It was one of the sweetest kisses she had ever tasted. No tongue, just a tenderness that said he cared.

Did he really care? He had certainly shown how much Maggie meant to him. The woman was free.

Freedom.

Fallon closed her eyes and savored the thought. When she opened her eyes it was to meet Adrian's intensity.

"It's late and you need to feed before we turn in." He tipped his head, baring his neck.

"Will it be okay?" she asked, knowing that he supplied Maggie with sustenance, not to mention her, earlier.

"I fed plenty before I came to her room."

The vein that bulged in his throat looked so inviting. She snuggled close, inhaling the earthy scent that was all Adrian. Lightly, she nuzzled his neck and the artery seemed to swell in anticipation. She hesitated only a moment before parting her lips and sinking her fangs into his flesh. Immediately, she felt the rush of his power surging through her veins.

"Ahhh…baby," he murmured. His arms closed around her and his cock hardened against her belly. With a slight boost, he raised her so that her legs slipped around his waist. She continued to feed as he thrust inside her once more. At the same time he began to move, walking toward the staircase that would lead them down below.

With a swipe of her tongue she closed the wound, then rested her head against his shoulder. A heavy sigh pushed from her mouth.

The rich scent of soil greeted her. The earth had already been prepared for them. With ease Adrian stepped into the hole and lay upon his back, taking her down with him to lie atop him.

"Sleep, darlin'. We have a big day ahead of us tomorrow."

Fallon didn't have to pretend that she didn't know what he was talking about.

Damn it. That was one conversation she wasn't looking forward to.

Chapter Ten

Fallon's mental scream could have wakened the dead. In fact, the bloodcurdling shriek had scared the shit out of Adrian as he jackknifed to a sitting position from their bed of soil, spraying it into the air. His thoughts were to hunt as she slept. Instead he drew her slumbering body into his arms. Perspiration glistened on her skin as he rose and made his way to the stairs. Her face twisted in agony. The bitter stench of fear rose from her pores as she trembled.

Halfway up the stairs, on a gasp her eyes flew open. She started to struggle, releasing desperate cries as he tightened his grip, so she wouldn't fall out of his arms. Tears raced down her cheeks. Her cries were sharp and filled with anguish.

"Fallon," he whispered. Then he kissed her forehead. "It's me, darlin'."

When she realized who held her, her body went limp. She wrapped her arms around his neck and released a flood of emotion, deep, wrenching sobs that felt like they were reaching into his chest and tearing out his heart.

He couldn't image what she had been through, but he was damn well going to find out tonight.

By the time they reached his above ground bedroom, he had called upon the elements to cleanse them both. Her tears had dried.

Her eyes were reddened and swollen from her outburst. She appeared embarrassed, refusing to meet his gaze.

Gently, he laid her upon the bed and she cried out in pain, moving quickly to her side and off her back.

"Ow…" She frowned letting her disapproval be known as their eyes met. "The soreness isn't gone. Why?" Accusation burned bright in the depths of her eyes.

"A reminder—"

"Fuck your reminder." She groaned, shifting her leg. "This isn't funny any more."

"Fallon, it wasn't funny to begin with. Bottom line, honey, you'll heal like any human would heal after a spanking."

Disbelief widened her eyes. "You're kidding?"

"No. I'm not."

Her scowl gradually softened. He sensed when she reached inside herself to counteract what he had done. Frustration returned quickly. "Well, shit." She eased off the bed, carefully. Again, she glared at him and for a moment he thought she'd say more.

Adrian knew better than to show his amusement. There were no marks on the beautiful skin that she quickly covered with a silky full skirt of emerald-green that rose mid-thigh. He knew she wore no panties and the thought gave him an immediate hard-on.

She glanced at his rigid form and he could read her thoughts. "*No fuckin' way, buster.*"

He did laugh this time.

"Funny. Ha-ha," she blustered, before covering her breasts with a soft peasant blouse that hung off her shoulders. The cute little cowboy boots she wore finished the outfit. As she strolled over to the window, the short skirt teased him, swaying and caressing her ass.

Man, did he want a piece of that. He ran his fingers through his hair. Since it was clear he wasn't getting any lovin' he, too, quickly dressed in boots, blue jeans and a cotton shirt. "Ready to talk?"

Lights from the arena and several other buildings lit the night and flooded the room as she pulled the drapes back. "Adrian, you're better off just letting me leave." She stared blindly out the window. "If I go now I can make up some ground."

His boots clicked across the wooden floor as he walked toward her. "I told you, you're not leaving."

She turned to confront him. "You can't make me stay."

He narrowed his eyes. "Try me." His tone left no room for argument.

She still didn't get it. There was no way she was leaving unless she had a damn good reason.

With a shake of her head, she said, "You think last night was bad." He didn't care for her silence or the way her face lost all color. "You haven't seen anything like the demon chasing me." Glancing around the room, she looked like a caged animal ready to bolt if the door opened.

"C'mon, let's sit down."

She huffed. "I'd rather stand thanks to you."

"Then let's take a walk. We can swing by and see how Maggie is doing before we leave the house." Adrian attempted to grasp her hand, but she jerked it back. He didn't know if it was because she was still upset about the spanking or if anyone touching her right now would receive the same response. Clearly someone had messed her up.

Their footsteps echoed down the hallway. Standing outside of Maggie's bedroom, Adrian rapped lightly on the door.

"What'da ya' want," Tucker barked through the closed door.

"It's me," Adrian said and pushed open the door. He first glanced toward the bed, but it was empty. Then he glanced at Tucker. He frowned, nodding toward the corner where Maggie sat cradling herself. Her face tucked in her arms.

"She won't even let me come near her. She needs to feed," Tucker complained. The scowl on his face may have been taken as anger, but Adrian knew Tucker was beyond concerned. He had bedded Maggie down with him last night, never allowing her out of his sight. Adrian knew this because throughout the early morning he had kept tabs on her.

"I'll do it," Adrian said and received a glare from Tucker. "You're already in hot water with me—don't push it." Tucker backed off, but he wasn't happy.

When Adrian got within six feet of Maggie she panicked, fear twisted her features. She started to kick and scream, fighting an invisible demon that didn't exist.

A hand on his arm made him pause. "Let me try," Fallon asked.

When Adrian nodded Tucker said, "You're *not* going to let her feed Maggie." It wasn't issued as a question.

Adrian snapped his head around. He knew his eyes glowed red. His fangs had dropped, displaying as his lip curled into a snarl. The low, menacing warning he issued in the form of a growl made Tucker take a step backward.

Misty-eyed, Fallon turned to face Tucker. "No. I won't feed her. She's been through so much already. I wouldn't wish what I have following me on anyone. Let me just talk to her." She continued on toward Maggie.

Kneeling beside Maggie, Fallon whispered, "You're free." Maggie raised her tortured gaze to met Fallon's. The soft smile Fallon gave her seemed to calm Maggie as her grip around her shoulders relaxed. "Sweetie, you're free and he'll never come looking for you again."

"Really?" Maggie's voice was weak, childlike and barely audible.

Fallon nodded. "It's true. Now close your eyes and take a deep breath."

Maggie appeared a little hesitant, but finally her eyelids drifted shut. She inhaled deeply.

"Freedom," Fallon whispered, inhaling deeply. The serene look that briefly flashed across her face gave him the impression she could really smell it. The strained emotion in her voice made Adrian's chest tighten. "Isn't it wonderful?"

When Maggie eyes opened, she said, "You?"

Fallon sucked her bottom lip in her mouth and bit down. "Yes." She slid carefully onto her hip and reached out to hold Maggie's hand. "Never again will he hurt you." Fallon's face tightened in obvious anguish as she fought for control. Still several tears rolled down her cheek. She swallowed hard, plainly fighting with her own invisible demons. "Now you have to let the people who love you help so you can recover. You need to feed."

"You would offer your blood?" Maggie asked.

"No. You don't want my blood. But Tucker or Adrian—"

"Adrian." Evidently, Maggie responded too quickly for Tucker's comfort. A low, quiet sound from deep inside him expressed his disapproval.

"Give her time," Adrian murmured to Tucker, before he headed toward Maggie. Keeping his distance, he knelt and extended his arm. "Drink, Maggie, and grow strong."

Fear was a difficult creature to vanquish. She stared at the blue veins in his wrist and swallowed, hard. He could sense her hunger and need. She glanced at Fallon.

"Take what he offers," Fallon encouraged. "You can trust Adrian. Let him help you."

Fallon must have said the right words, because Maggie cradled Adrian's wrist in her palms. Her incisors dropped, she dipped her head, and he felt the sharp sting as her fangs pierced his flesh.

Warm and wet, her tongue skimmed across his skin closing the wound. She raised her head and looked him into his eyes. "Thank you, Adrian."

With a palm he cupped her cheek. "Maggie, you know I'll always take care of you."

The door slammed as Tucker left the room.

Adrian stood and offered Maggie his hand. She accepted it and rose. He led her over to the bed. "Sleep now and we'll come back and check on you later." She slipped beneath the covers and he tucked the bedding beneath her form. Then he tapped her on the nose. "Don't let the bed-bugs bite."

When he turned back around Fallon was already standing. Face haggard, she looked drained of all energy. He gathered her into his arms, holding her close.

"Who?" he asked.

"Pedro Chavez."

"*Ahhh…shit!*"

Adrian didn't need to say anything more. The expression on his face spoke loudly. Clearly, he knew Chavez. The *ahhh…shit* comment meant he also knew the bastard was bad news.

Get ready for your walking papers.

Her shoulders slumped. God, she was tired. Everywhere she turned she ran smack-dab into a wall. Just once she wanted to find someone willing to help. But she knew the price would be too high to pay. Chavez would kill anyone who attempted to help her.

Besides this was her battle.

She glanced at Maggie, thankful the woman's nightmares were finally over. Fallon took a breath of courage and faced Adrian. "Thank you."

With just a couple steps he closed the distance between them. "For what?" Warm palms slid around her biceps as he pulled her to him. His chest pressed to hers felt good, too good.

In an effort to evade the tears building behind her eyes, she closed them. Maybe she could have said her good-byes without a show of emotion, but not with him touching her. She stepped back out of his arms, before raising her eyelids. It was difficult, but she forced a smile on her lips and took a breath of courage.

She shrugged one shoulder. "Hey. It was good while it lasted." The façade was a strain to hold onto. If she didn't get out of there and fast, he'd see right through her.

A look of confusion brushed his handsome features. "Sounds like you're saying good-bye."

She countered with, "No time like the present to hit the road."

He shook his head. Exasperation pushed his gaze to the ceiling. "You are one stubborn woman. What part of 'you're not leaving me' didn't you get?"

Stunned, she stumbled as he pulled her back into his arms. He rested his chin on her head.

"Adrian—"

"Shhh…not here. Let's take a walk." With his arm around her shoulders he guided her out of Maggie's room.

Tucker leaned against the hallway wall outside her door, hat in his hands. For a vampire, Fallon would have thought he would be more presentable. His hair was mussed and he had a day old beard. He looked haggard, as if he hadn't slept.

"Is she asleep?" he asked, rotating his hat in his hands.

"Yeah," Adrian said. "You okay?"

Tucker released a short spurt of laughter. "Man, I fucked up."

"Won't argue with you there, pal." Adrian laid a reassuring hand on Tucker's arm. "Give her time. Then tell her."

Tucker wagged his head, pausing before he said, "Sorry, man."

Fallon couldn't help noticing that a silent message exchanged between men. Adrian's face was stern. Tucker appeared thoroughly chagrined, as he pushed away from the wall and entered Maggie's bedroom.

As she and Adrian continued down the hall, Fallon asked, "What was that all about?"

He glanced down at her. "What?"

"Maggie and Tucker?"

"Maggie came to me a couple years ago battered and broken, skittish as a new colt. She took a chance. Reached out to Tucker. Tucker wasn't ready. Maggie withdrew."

They entered the vacant living room. "So now he's ready?" Fallon could hear several voices coming from the kitchen.

Adrian cocked his head, listening. His gaze fell on her. "Give the man a break."

"Break?" She released a mocking breath. "He needs his ass kicked. Uh…are you gonna tan his hide?"

A spark lit his eyes. A devilish grin tipped his mouth, but before he could answer he pushed open the door leading to the kitchen and they entered.

All eyes turned to them. Sally was kneading dough for tomorrow's bread. The smell of yeast filled the large room. Gary was sitting at the large picnic table before the window that looked out over Adrian's land. Several other men, vampires she recognized from the barbeque, were sitting at the table, too. Cougar and Briar rose and came immediately to Adrian's side. Quiet words were exchanged.

"Fallon." Adrian nodded toward the table. "Take a load off. I'll be right back." He and the other two men started toward the backdoor.

The first bit of pressure on Fallon's sore ass as she sat down had her jumping to her feet, releasing a tight squeal.

Hand on the doorknob, Adrian pulled to a stop and glanced over his shoulder at her. She pinned him with a scowl. His deep chuckle was nothing like the knowing smirks that went between Cougar and Briar.

Dammit. Did everyone know?

"How's Maggie?" Sally asked, drawing her attention, as her ass continued to throb. The woman's strong hands pushed and mixed the dough laid out on a butcher block surface dusted with flour. "Tucker wouldn't let any of us near her."

"She's sleeping." Fallon had made bread a couple times. She couldn't help smiling at the memory. It wasn't one of her greatest moments, but it had been fun cooking with her daughter. Anyone who could actually get the stuff to rise deserved a pat on the back.

"And you?" Sally was too perceptive.

Fallon was sure she was flushing all shades of red. "Sore."

Sally grinned as she stared into the bowl in front of her. "Our boy doesn't like to be disobeyed."

Fallon resisted the urge to rub her ass. "You're telling me."

Sally chuckled, as did the men at the table.

Fallon grew closer to Sally. "Does everyone know?"

The older woman's hands stilled. Her eyes were bright with amusement. "Honey, you two were broadcasting it worldwide."

"Well, *shit*. Excuse me." Fallon felt like crawling out of the kitchen. Instead she held her head high and waltzed out the back door. When she was alone she covered her face with her palms and released a muffled giggle.

Embarrassing? Yes. But she also had to admit that while in the throes of passion the experience had been the hottest she had ever felt. Just the thought of Adrian, the masterful way he wielded her body, aroused her. Already her nipples were tightening, her breasts growing heavy.

Truth be known—she'd do it again in a heartbeat.

She leaned lightly on the hitching post just outside the door.

Artificial lighting brightened the yard. In the distance she could see activity in the arena. Voices rose. The sounds of hooves beating the ground raised the dusty smell of dirt in the air. Curious, Fallon headed toward the noise.

Three 50 gallon barrels were laid out in a triangular form. Crystal, the brunette vampire she had seen at the barbeque last night, sat tall upon a yellowish-gray mare. The woman's long legs were clad in a pair of light blue fitted jeans. She wore a long-sleeve western shirt and boots and a cowboy hat to match. The buckskin snorted and reared back on its hind legs. When the animal's front legs touched the ground her powerful hindquarters bunched and sprang, as she lunged forward. It was a thing of beauty to watch Crystal and horse glide around each barrel, in a clover-leaf pattern, and then high-tail it back.

The roar from the crowd sitting upon the two sets of bleachers located outside the arena said Crystal did well. Once again human and vampire mingled. Laughter and camaraderie were all around Fallon.

It was a strange world Adrian had built for himself and his people, but it was a world she would give anything to be a part of—well, until it was time to join her daughter.

The reflection was bittersweet as thoughts of Adrian invaded her mind.

Chapter Eleven

A light breeze played with the hem of Fallon's short emerald-green skirt. The silky material fluttered softly, rising and falling, but never revealing what Adrian knew hid beneath. Just the thought of those smooth ass cheeks made his hands itch, his cock harden. Long legs were accented by a pair of white cowboy boots. She leaned on the metal piping fence of the arena, her arms folded on the second to the top rung. Her chin rested on her arms as she watched Doreen rein her Palomino gelding around the barrels. The horse's ivory mane and tail were a beautiful contrast flowing against its cream-colored body in action.

As Lita, a redheaded gal from town, entered the arena preparing to ride, Cougar said, "We sat at Little Tavern for over an hour and no one mentioned anything strange about last night. I think we're alright." He brushed his braid aside and set his straw cowboy hat back on his head. "Think there'll be retaliation?"

Briar turned away long enough to watch Lita's bay mare fly around the first barrel. Sadness darkened the man's eyes.

"Think anyone will miss Dominic?" Adrian asked, already knowing the answer.

"No," Cougar responded dryly.

Clapping from the audience and the squeal from the wildcat upon the horse as she finished her ride had Briar frowning. "Damn woman's gonna kill herself," he mumbled beneath his breath.

Temperament and emotion were not something Adrian expected from Briar. He was usually somewhat indifferent. Even as he and Adrian fought Dominic and his minions Briar never once faltered. He killed swiftly and without remorse.

"We've got another problem." Adrian's gaze drifted back to Fallon. With a quick flick of his finger he stirred the air so that it rushed beneath her skirt, lifting it to give him a birds-eye view of her delicious ass. Just as he thought, she wore no panties.

Her tight squeal put a smile on his face. Blood rushed his groin. Arms flailing, she fought to control the skirt, but not before he got several more eyefuls.

Cougar snickered. "If she knows it's you doing that you're dead."

Shit! His friend saw that.

"Problem?" Briar asked, though his sights were pinned on the people rolling the barrels out of the arena, while others started setting up for bull riding. A smaller fence was resurrected within the arena to control where the Brahmin roamed. Several of Adrian's own men would control the animals with their powers, if need be. He wanted no one hurt—not on his property.

"It seems that Maggie isn't the only woman being pursued." Before Adrian could say more the chute gate flew open and out came Lita on a big, black bull.

"Sonofabitch!" Briar yelled as he took off running toward the arena where the woman from town tested her luck.

Lita was tucked close to the large hump over the animal's shoulders. One hand in the air, she raked the beast's shoulders with her spurs. Her long red hair whipped back and forth, up and down, with each swift movement of the bull.

One second she was seated, the next airborne.

Adrian felt Briar catch her with his magic, but intentionally release it when she was about three feet above the ground. She landed on her ass with a dull thud.

Briar was the first one to reach her, which necessitated the need to plant memories in the humans that he had been in the arena all along.

As he jerked her to her feet, she hummed, "What a rush…" Hands wrapped around her biceps, he gave her a little shake. "What?" she asked.

"Nothing," he growled, releasing her quickly. "Stay off the bulls."

She grinned, wrinkling her nose as she cocked her head. "Broncos?"

"No broncos," he snapped, tugging his hat further down in front of his face.

"Briar…" The little vixen's voice was low and seductive. "Then what do you want me to ride?"

"Fuck," he swore, before pivoting and stomping off.

"Anytime," she tittered softly.

"Okay. Anyone else find that a little strange?" Adrian asked, turning back around to face Cougar.

Briar was heading their way and he didn't look happy, not if the dirt he was stirring up with each heavy footfall was an indication. The dusty scent filled the air.

"It seems quite a few of our menfolk are having women problems these days." Cougar winked. "You were mentioning a certain problem in particular, before Lita yanked Briar's chain."

"She didn't yank my chain. And what does this have to do with me? I was just following the boss's order. No one gets hurt. Besides we were talking about a problem. Yeah. What the hell is your problem, Boss?" Briar's rapid and steady outburst had both Adrian and Cougar speechless.

Was there something in the water? The air? Or blood?

If Adrian didn't know better he would have thought it was vampire mating season, if there were such a thing. Because something was definitely wrong. Tucker was in a snit. Briar was acting strangely, and the damn love-bug had bitten Adrian, too.

Bottom line he was crazy about Fallon. But he wasn't crazy about her problem.

"Pedro Chavez," he said with distaste.

"I know that name." Briar pondered for a moment and then his face hardened. "Oh, yeah. I know the bastard."

"Who is he?" Cougar asked.

"Bad news." Adrian removed his hat and ran his fingers through his hair. "Like Fallon said, 'You think last night was bad?' Let me put it this way. What Maggie went through was a piece of cake to what I suspect Fallon has experienced." Adrian ground his teeth together to keep his fury at bay.

Cougar's face paled. "Jesus, Adrian." Cougar had seen the condition Maggie came to them in. It was something a man never forgot. The brutality had been appalling. Her stories of rape and torture were beyond imaginable.

"I haven't got all the details, but Fallon's frightened. She's ready to run." Adrian had been able to smell the bitter scent of fear on her since Maggie's attack. He could feel the war that raged in Fallon's mind, thinking she was in this alone.

"You gonna let her go?" Briar shot him a look that said, "Remember, women mess with a man's head."

His friend's words and his hopeful expression didn't set well with Adrian. He narrowed his eyes on Briar. "Never."

"Well, then I guess we best be getting ready for Armageddon, because I can guarantee that this will be a battle between good and evil before Judgment Day—if we make it that far." Briar removed his hat and struck it against his leg a couple times.

"That bad?" Cougar asked.

"That bad," Adrian confirmed. "I need someone to locate Chavez. I want to know where he is at all times."

"Just follow the blood trail," Briar added dryly.

"Then we need to prepare. I don't want Chavez getting past my guard like Dominic did." Adrian had been too wrapped up in Fallon, not paying attention, or he would have felt something when Dominic touched ground. That wasn't going to happen again.

This was Adrian's land. He cared for it—in return it spoke to him.

"What the hell?" Fallon fought the gust of air that tickled her ass, raising her skirt, again. The wind hadn't been blowing when she left the house and oddly enough seemed to come and go sporadically. She'd change into a pair of jeans or put panties on, but the soreness from Adrian's punishment had yet to disappear.

From where she stood she had a great view of the chutes. She watched one cowboy after another tossed on their ass. This cowboy world was a strange one indeed. How much fun could there be in climbing up on a big, hairy, smelly beast only to be tossed right back on your butt? Not to mention the danger. A swift kick against one's head by a thousand pounds of pure fury would certainly make sure that person never rode or even stood again.

Warm palms settled on her bare shoulders, startling her. She glanced back to find Adrian behind her. His thumb moved seductively over the bare skin of her shoulders where her peasant sleeves hung. With a step forward he spooned her back. His firm body against every inch of her form. One particular part appeared to be harder than the rest, bringing a grin to her face.

He pressed his right hand to her thigh and inched it upward.

"We have an audience," she reminded him, inhaling a woodsy aftershave. Damn. He smelled good enough to eat.

The crowd in the bleachers roared as Cougar completed his eight second ride on a horse the announcer called Hellfire. The rodeo was two days away and Fallon could tell that everyone was ready for it to get underway. Men and women alike were lining up to ride.

"Would you like me to fuck you here? In front of an audience?" His wicked question tightened her nipples with sharp tingles. The hand on her thigh moved higher beneath her skirt. She couldn't control the shiver that assaulted her. The hairs on her neck sprang to life as if they were electrically charged.

"Stop it now or I'll take you up on it." She giggled. It felt good to laugh, even knowing that she had not yet spoken to Adrian about Chavez. Reliving each morning what had happened to Christy was agonizing, but to share it with Adrian somehow felt insurmountable. She hadn't told a single soul about her daughter.

From where they stood no one could actually see Adrian's hand. From the back he sheltered her, from the front her skirt was full enough no one would notice. The only way anyone would see what he was doing was if the person actually stood to the right of them.

With a single finger he traced the seam where her thigh and hip met, moving slowly toward the nest of hair hidden beneath.

"Adrian," she warned, but scooted her booted feet further apart.

"Hey, you two." Crystal sauntered up to them, thankfully on the opposite side of Fallon's raised skirt. "Maggie doing okay?"

"Hu-huh—" Oh God. This couldn't be happening.

"She'll be fine in time," Adrian assured. The devil threaded his fingers through her pubes. His finger was dangerously close to her swollen clit.

"Adrian?" She tensed beneath his touch.

"Darlin', relax. Enjoy." He gave a gentle yank on her short-hairs.

Relax? Enjoy? He wouldn't!

He did.

With a slip of his finger he buried it deep inside her. A rush of moisture greeted him. This was beyond embarrassing.

"Relax." There was laughter in his voice. *"I've shut down all our links, but the one between us."*

"Stop it, Adrian." There was desperation in hers.

"Relax, or Crystal will know exactly what I'm doing and what I'm gonna do to you."

"Nice ride, Crystal." He gazed at the brunette dressed in red, while he slowly moved his finger in and out of Fallon's wet pussy. "It looks like Jewel is working out for you."

Crystal flashed Adrian a bright smile. Her eyes sparkled. "She's a nice horse. Thank you."

Another finger joined the first giving Fallon an even fuller feeling between her thighs.

"For what?" Adrian asked. *"Can you smell your arousal?"*

Fallon's belly tightened. Yes, she could smell her own heat, but could Crystal?

"*I want to taste you.*" His admission almost made Fallon groan aloud. It was hard enough to keep her hips from riding his hand.

"Thank you for Jewel. She's a remarkable animal." Crystal's smile was radiant. "Are you enjoying your stay here, Fallon?"

"Yes," she hissed, before adding, "very much."

When Adrian's finger found her clit, Fallon gripped the bar in front of her. Automatically, she slightly bent her knees, sinking down into the pressure moving circle after circle around her swollen nub. Fallon rode the edge of her climax, praying that when she came she didn't scream.

"*That's it, darlin'.*" His mental voice was so damn sexy it set off a tremor through her.

Crystal's brows tugged together as she glanced askance at Fallon.

"Are you riding again tonight?" Adrian said quickly, drawing her attention.

"No. Not tonight."

"Hey, Crystal," some cowboy called to her. He raised his hand in the air and motioned her over to where a group of people stood.

She waved at the guy. "I better go." She smiled sweetly up at Adrian. "He's dinner."

The moment Crystal was out of earshot, Adrian ground his hips against Fallon's ass and whispered, "Come for me."

Fallon jerked once and shattered into a mass of sensations. All the while Adrian continued his assault, wringing out every response he could. Colors exploded behind her eyelids. The tension tight inside her released, soaring from her as if he freed it with his touch. She gasped as the incredible feeling took hold of her. The sense of rising was abruptly splintered with another unexpected orgasm that gave her the feeling of falling.

"Adrian. Hold me," she cried out, unsure whether she could continue to stand as one after another aftershocks rippled, relentlessly clenching and releasing every muscle in her body.

Within seconds, she found herself spun around and in his embrace. She flung her arms around his neck, knowing that her skirt barely covered her ass, but she didn't care.

"I need to fuck you." She heard the hunger in his voice shadowed by regret. "But I need to feed first. If I come to you in this condition I wouldn't do either of us any favor."

Before she slipped her arms from around his neck, she tried her legs, shuffled her feet. She was good to go. "Lead the way."

"You're not going anywhere." She caught the edge of disquiet in his voice.

"Why?"

"Go to the house—my bedroom. I'll meet you there as quickly as I can."

She had to admit that his caution was a little scary. "Adrian, I refuse to hide—"

He cupped her face silencing her with a kiss. When he released her she said, "You can't use a kiss to shut me up every time."

She loved the way he smiled. It brightened his entire face and made his eyes shine.

"Try me." He popped her on the ass.

She squealed jumping away from him. "Ouch. Why'd you do that?"

"Just a reminder to obey me." All playfulness disappeared. His voice developed a firmness she knew not to test. "Now wait for me in our room."

Ours? Did he say *our room?*

Chapter Twelve

Adrian walked the grounds around the house. After watching to make sure Fallon made it to the house, he had gone into town and found substance from two strangers. Before he left he had to make sure the safeguards he and his people had established were in place. Now he was checking them once more as he walked the perimeter.

His magic was strong. The problem was that he didn't know how strong Chavez's magic was. Only meeting the man once—once being enough—Adrian had quickly wanted to be out of the man's presence.

Chavez was a sick son of a bitch.

Anger rose quickly and without warning. What had Chavez done to Fallon? In reality, Adrian really didn't want to know. Already he could feel the hatred for the vampire grow, a slow burning flame that needed one good dose of fuel to erupt into a full blown forest fire.

Rage didn't travel well into battle. He had seen that fact with Tucker. His friend would have surely died if he, Cougar and Briar had not stopped him from lunging headfirst into war with Dominic.

Gravel crunched beneath Adrian's feet as he walked on the driveway where a black truck was parked just outside the house. He leaned against it, looking into the cloud-shrouded sky.

He didn't care for the way the land trembled. He listened to the serenade of crickets, the trickle of a small stream that ran in the back of the house, and the roar of a black bear in the distance. It wasn't clear to him if his sense of unease came from the storm brewing or maybe the earth itself knew they were in a race against time to vanquish another evil from this world.

With a deep breath he inhaled the smell of oncoming rain and pine. The scent of chewing tobacco rose. Gary was near and so was the stroke of midnight. Fallon would be waiting for him.

Adrian had faced plenty of trials throughout the years, but tonight he felt burdened by his responsibilities. What if he couldn't stop Chavez from getting his hands on Fallon? What about his people? The innocent humans who weren't even aware of the evil that walked among them? He couldn't imagine the damage that the battle would wreak upon this beautiful country.

There was so much at stake.

"It don't do you any good to worry." Gary spat on the ground, as he moved from behind a pine tree. He walked slightly hunched over as if his back were hurting him tonight. "Son, you do the best you can. You always have since I've known you. No one expects more than that."

Not true. Adrian expected more.

For maybe the first time in his immortal life he was looking forward to the next hundred years with Fallon by his side.

"Gary, you ever want someone so badly you could taste it?" Adrian asked.

"Yep. My Sally." He spat again on the ground. "Funny thing about love. A man like you can control the wind and the lightning from the sky, but you can't control who you fall in love with."

Love?

There was a long silence. Gravel popped as Gary shuffled his feet. "Best be getting inside before it starts to rain." Then he paused. "Son, if she's the one don't be letting her go." With a quiet grunt he straightened his crooked form and headed for the house.

Adrian would give anything if it were that easy. By rights Fallon belonged to another. To have her, he would have to kill Pedro Chavez.

⟡

When Adrian entered the bedroom Fallon was standing by the window, her hand gripping the curtain as she turned to face him. Wariness rimmed her eyes. Had she watched him as he surveyed the perimeters of the property? Did she doubt his ability to protect her?

Music played softly in the background. The whine of a steel guitar and the beat of a drum joined with the haunting sounds of a bass guitar as Josh Turner started to sing. It seemed appropriate that his song entitled "Your Man" was the choice. When the artist sang "turn the lights down low," Adrian dimmed the lights, allowing the blaze from the fireplace to illuminate the room in soft shadows. Then he crooked his index finger, calling Fallon to his side.

As she approached him, her hips swayed seductively. Her dark hair hung loosely, flowing by her sides. She still wore the short emerald-green skirt, the white peasant blouse that bared her shoulders. The white cowboy boots made her legs look long and luscious.

"Adrian?"

He placed his finger against her full lips. Then he took her into his arms and together they moved across the floor. Her body melted into his as their feet shuffled to the beat of the song. He held her close, aware of how her breathing hitched when he pressed his hips to hers.

His cock was hard and getting firmer each time she rubbed against him.

Earlier he had fed, but having her near, touching her, and smelling her womanly scent drove him crazy. He needed to taste her sweet blood as he brought her to climax over and over again.

With slow, steady steps she swayed to the beat like she was making love to the music. He swung her gently around and then back into his arms, each time drawing her hard against him, so she knew just how much she turned him on—how much he desired her.

As their hips and feet shifted from place to place, he guided her arms above her head. "Keep them up," he said, before he shoved his hands beneath the bottom of her peasant blouse. Her skin was warm to the touch as he placed his palms at her waist. It made him fucking hot to feel her hips undulate beneath his hands, knowing that he would soon be inside her, feeling the rhythm and rock of her hips against him. Pulse speeding, he smoothed his hands over her belly, the ridges of her ribs, to finally cup her breasts.

She whimpered lightly, urging him to roll the peaks between his fingers. Her eyes were half-shuttered, her body still moving with his to the music. With a quick yank he slipped her blouse over her head and tossed it aside. When he drew her near this time he wrapped his arms around her body, his palms caressing her naked back.

"My turn," she whispered, bringing her arms down to tug at his shirt to dislodge it from his jeans. Hip to hip, she leaned back to give herself enough room to undo each button.

The touch of her hands against his abdomen almost threw him into meltdown. God, he wanted to strip her naked, lay her down and lose himself inside her. The glide of his shirt off his shoulders brought him that much closer.

When they came together again it was as it should be—flesh to flesh.

As the song ended and another one began, he murmured, "Are you wet for me, darlin'?" His palms slipped down her back, flipped up her skirt and grasped her ass.

"*Yes*," she cried out.

"Do you want me?" he asked with a slow southern draw.

Fallon was more than wet and ready. She was drenched with desire. Breasts heavy, her nipples throbbed to feel his warm, moist mouth on them, licking and sucking. As he spun her around she dipped low, so that when he pulled her back into his embrace she sensually drew her chest up his firm body.

Dark hunger turned his eyes a liquid gold. They were mesmerizing. Hypnotic. Their power seemed to reduce her to almost a lethargic state. She was drowning in his passion, eager to quench his thirst.

Thoughts past this moment—this man—were almost nonexistent.

Unmercifully, he stoked the flame burning brightly inside her as he ground his hips to hers. The way he held her, his palm pressed to that sensitive spot at the small of her back as he commanded her across the floor, was masterful.

Strong and confident, he led—she followed.

Fallon wanted Adrian with every beat of her heart. He was a weakness she feared she could never get enough of.

"Too many clothes." His deep, sexy growl moved across her skin roughly, making every nerve ending sensitive and raw. A sharp tingle hissed, raising the hairs on her arms as her boots and skirt dissolved. The next minute he was as naked as she.

Music soft and low, Gary Allen's "Dancing With Nothing On But The Radio" took on a whole new meaning. She had never felt anything as erotic as their bare forms moving to the beat of the song, the freedom in a turn, or the coming together of their bodies.

"Fuck me." Her low, thick moan was a plea. Unable to resist touching him, her hand wedged between them to cup and stroke his stiff erection.

The minute her fingers closed around his cock, he gasped. Crimson drops of blood beaded as his sharp, white fangs appeared in his mouth. The rich scent was heavenly, triggering her incisors to emerge. Her mouth salivated. The taste of her own blood lay upon her tongue. His essence called to her, waiting to be sampled.

Fallon had never seen anything as sexy as the hunger raging upon his face or his body fully aroused as she stroked him from balls to tip. His hips undulated against her hand, increasing the rhythm. When his palms settled on her shoulders, exerted pressure so that her knees bent, she knew exactly what he wanted—and she was more than happy to oblige.

As she sank further down to the floor, she pressed her lips to his chest, kissing a path across his heated skin. His grip tightened when she dipped her tongue into his bellybutton. Her other hand cradled his testicles. Gently, she fondled the two oval glands, pulling and stretching the soft skin of his scrotum.

"Now." His voice was firm and demanding. Her belly tightened with his command. "Fuck me with your hot, wet mouth—*now*." She loved the tension in his voice. It meant she was affecting him as much as he did her.

With her hand still gripping the base of his cock, she licked the length of him. A tremor rippled through him. He hissed, sucking air between his clenched teeth. The points of his fangs dimpled his bottom lip. A lock of hair fell over one eye as he looked down at her.

"Yeah. *Ohhh…*" he breathed. "More." Fire burned in the depths of his gaze riveted on her lips. When she took him into her mouth, his pupils dilated. "God…" The single word came out on a throaty groan. "Deeper— More—" His mouth parted, as his hips thrust forward, driving him to the back of her throat. "Fuck. You feel so good."

A swirl of her tongue over the small slit at the crown won her a taste of his salty pre-come. When her eyelids closed his hands moved from her shoulders to her hair, fingers curling and yanking her head back, so that her neck arched and her eyes widened.

"Watch me fuck your mouth." He pumped in and out, slipping between her lips, filling her mouth with every inch of his cock.

Saliva built in her mouth. She swallowed, the action making him jerk.

"God, I don't want to come. Not now." The taut expression on his face said he was fighting his climax.

She smiled around her mouthful of cock. She had every intention of making him lose control. She swallowed again.

"Dammit, baby, don't do that unless you want a mouthful of come."

She swallowed again.

Adrian moved so quickly Fallon didn't know what was happening. The next thing she realized her back was pressed against the cool wall of the bedroom. He clasped her ass in his strong hands, raising her and spreading her thighs wide. "Lock your legs around my waist." Wrapping her arms around his neck, she complied. Then he buried his firm erection deep inside her.

With pounding thrusts he rocked against her cradle, filling her with an incredible fullness. She wanted to cry out from the pleasure. "Harder."

Her head bounced against the wall as he drove harder—deeper inside her. The slap of their flesh coming together made her inner muscles spasm. The sweet scent of sex caressed her nose. There was something primitive in his sexy, deep sounds he made as he slammed into her body over and over.

As the coil inside her drew tighter, she screamed, "Harder. Fuck me, harder."

He moved with preternatural speed, ripping her from the wall and jerking her to the bed so that she lay upon her stomach. Before she could inhale his hands pushed beneath her, palms pressing against her abdomen as he raised her ass, parted her slit and entered her.

"Oh, God," she murmured. His rigid cock struck the back of her cervix. She braced her palms on the soft comforter, raising herself so that next time he shoved his hips forward, she met him halfway. Again and again, he drove unrelentingly between her thighs, never relaxing or easing his strokes.

The pleasure/pain was unreal as he struck her sore ass each time he slid between her swollen flesh. She couldn't breathe. Her body tensed, tightening into one big knot preparing to unravel.

Fast, but gently, he rolled her over to her back, driving her further up the bed as their bodies came together again.

"Come for me, darlin'." Like silk gliding over polished marble, his deep, sexy voice led her to the precipice, but it was his fangs piercing the soft swell of her breast that pushed her over the edge.

She threw back her head and screamed.

The prism of lights in her mind shattered and swirled, constantly changing in color and shape. She writhed beneath him uncontrollably. He continued to thrust in and out, hard and fast, between her legs. Her orgasm felt like it was ripped from her womb to course through her body—a burn that threatened to devour.

She felt hot—so very hot.

All she could think of was spontaneous combustion as the heat grew—abruptly exploding into another round of fiery sensations.

She arched beneath him. "Adrian!" Pleasure tore her asunder. To anchor herself she sank her incisors deep into his neck.

One more lunge and Adrian stilled. A loud roar permeated his head. Pain tightened his balls. The flames shooting down his erection curled his toes in the bedding. A resonant groan tore from somewhere deep in his throat. While she took his blood, her body squeezed his cock, again and again, milking him of his seed. The strain on his groin wouldn't let up. The pleasure so intense it left him breathless.

When the last bit of his come flowed into her body, she closed the wound at his neck. He heard her sated sigh. Loved the way she snuggled into his neck as she found comfort. Lightly, her fingertips danced over his back. Quick movements consisting of two lines that crossed over each other to form a cross. The next series of lines were short and wispy drawn in a crescent shape that feathered the top of the cross.

Adrian's heart stuttered.

Did she even realize what she was doing?

Fallon had drawn the pattern of unity—a mating sign meant to safeguard one's mate before he headed to battle.

"What are you doing?" he said and her hand stilled. He hadn't meant to sound so disconcerted.

She tensed beneath him. "I'm sorry." Hurt rang in her apology.

"It's okay." He rose above her, rolling to his side. "I just wanted to know what you were drawing."

"Nothing." A defensive tone rang in her voice. "I was tickling your back."

"Tickling?"

"Yeah. Like I used to do to Christy's ba—" Fallon went deathly quiet. Color drained from her face.

Obviously this was someone she didn't wish to talk about. He couldn't let her keep things bottled up inside. She had to learn to trust him—even with her secrets.

"Who's Christy?"

Indecision warred across her face running the gamut from fear to hope.

Her chest rose on an inhale. As she pushed the air from her lungs, she said, "My daughter."

That was one answer he hadn't expected. For a moment Adrian didn't know what to say. Slowly, he cleared his throat. "You have a daughter?"

Fallon raised her chin. Whether it was a defensive move or she fought to control her emotions, he wasn't sure. "Had a daughter." Her voice cracked.

Had? They were either estranged, maybe an ex-husband had guardianship due to Fallon's immortality or the child no longer lived. The thought that Fallon had been married didn't set well with him. "Where is she?"

"Dead." Her reply was nearly inaudible.

He waited for tears that didn't come. No wonder she had nightmares. "What happened to her?"

"Pedro Chavez." There was enough rancor pronounced in his name to melt steel.

Adrian reached for Fallon, needing to comfort her, but she withdrew climbing off the bed. Gracing him with her shapely back, he watched as a tremor rippled through her body.

When she turned to face him, her eyes were cloudy, cold and unemotional. Not once did she blink an eye, as she said, "I'm going to kill him." The chill in her tone left absolutely no doubt in Adrian's mind she meant every word.

Chapter Thirteen

Quietly, Adrian rose from the bed. Fallon stood like a statue. Her facial features hardened—her stance unyielding. Soft music continued to play in the background, but he doubted she was listening. The wooden floor was chilly beneath his bare feet as he stepped before her.

He reached out to her, but before his hands came into contact, she whispered, "Please. Don't touch me."

"Fallon—"

She closed her eyes as if tuning him out. He could feel her mental shields rise. If he wanted to penetrate them her strength was not enough to resist him. But he wouldn't invade her thoughts.

When she was ready—he'd be there for her.

A nervous tick started in the corner of her mouth. Her brows furrowed as the tick traveled to her chin making it lightly quiver. When her eyelids rose her lashes were spiked with tears. She ran her tongue between her dry lips. Again, she opened her mouth, then closed it tightly and shook her head.

"Breathe, darlin'."

The woman was holding on by a thread from the looks of it. He wanted to hold her, but he knew that it would be the catalyst that would surely lead to her breakdown.

So he silently waited, both of them naked, standing face to face.

Emotion glistened in her eyes as she looked up at him. "I brought him into our home after dating him a couple times. Just for coffee…" She took a ragged breath. He could see she held the air locked in her lungs, as she fought for composure. "I couldn't stop him." Her lips parted as she gulped down a hungry breath. "Her screams—" Pain twisted Fallon's beautiful features into a mass of agony that made his gut clench tight. As if she sought to stop herself from speaking of the terrifying event, her hands covered her mouth. Then she removed them, as she repeated, "I couldn't stop him."

Adrian saw red behind his eyelids. An innocent's death was hard to accept, but a child's…

Anger rushed through his veins hot and furious.

What Fallon and her child had gone through no one should ever have to bear. Chavez's cruelty had reached the ultimate in sadism. There was no way for a human—man or woman—to have stopped him.

Adrian tried to embrace her, but she stepped away. She had suffered in silence—suffered alone. He needed as much as wanted to hold her to chase the nightmare away.

Fallon's helplessness and guilt were raw, falling from her eyes in the form of tears. Tears he wanted to wipe away, but that was only physical. The ones that lay within her only time could erase.

Fallon's revenge, he thoroughly understood.

A snort sounded, as Fallon tried to pull herself together. Emotion continued to leak from her eyes. Her nose was reddening and began to run.

With a few footsteps he made it to the nightstand and retrieved a couple of tissues. Then he returned to Fallon, offering them to her, which she accepted.

The muscles in her neck tightened as she swallowed. "He-he t-tortured Christy— Drained her—" Her voice broke into short, gasping breaths as she looked away. "Blood. God. There was so much." Her fingers opened and closed rapidly. Pulse sped. "Her broken body—" Eyes rimmed red, they filled with a wild expression. "I-I watched. Couldn't move. It was as if my feet were rooted to the ground. My arms locked to my side. I didn't understand until later the compulsion Chavez placed upon me. I thought it was fear." Her sorrowful expression made his chest tighten. "He made me watch my baby die."

Fallon's body trembled with the force of an earthquake.

"Then he raped me." A little of her pain was washed away with a hint of rage surfacing that brightened her eyes. "Over and over again." Through clenched teeth she muttered, "Before he made me into what I am today."

"Son of a bitch." Adrian couldn't take any more. Grasping her arms, he forced her into his embrace and held her. He'd kill the bastard himself.

Fallon's forearms lay against his chest. Warm tears dampened his skin as she buried her head against his shoulder and cried.

Gently, he stroked her back. "Shhh… It's okay, darlin'."

With a quick jerk, she pushed from his arms. Her tears immediately. Pinched features skewed into a partial scowl, she countered sharply, "It will never be okay until he's dead."

"I didn't mean—"

Well fuck. Wrong choice of words.

Still in the grips of her fury, she said, "Teach me."

Adrian stiffened before he could help himself. "What?" God, he hoped she wasn't asking what he thought she was. Hadn't she learned by now that there was no way for her to defeat Chavez? Or was her pain too raw that it blinded her to the truth? Clearly, Fallon had seen and experienced way too much in her young life. A child's loss was a parent's worst fear.

With a single step she walked back into his arms, placing her palms flat on his chest. Fervent hunger stared up at him. "Teach me what I need to know to kill him." A glimpse of hope brightened her face. "Adrian, I'll do anything you ask of me. Just tell me what to do."

He cringed inwardly. Desperate pleas—or was it obsession he heard in her voice?

How was he supposed to answer her? Before he could stop himself, he shook his head. "Darlin'…"

The small gesture didn't go unnoticed. "You won't help me?" Fallon's shoulders drooped, as her hand fell from his chest to her side. She bowed her head.

With his finger beneath her chin, he brought her gaze to his. "I can't help you."

A whisper of sarcasm rose in her voice. "Can't or won't?"

"Can't," Adrian said firmly. He knew she didn't want to hear what he had to say, but she had to. "You will never obtain the power or knowledge to defeat Chavez. It's impossible. He made you. You live by his blood, which is his power. It flows through your veins. When he commands—you obey. Distance has been your only true friend."

She glowered. "But I know he can be killed. No one is truly immortal—not even Chavez."

"True. But a submissive can't kill his Master."

Her breath left her lungs in a single gush of air. "No…" Disheartened, she scrutinized him as if she searched for the lie that didn't exist in his statement.

"Then I don't have a choice." She spoke so softly he almost didn't hear her.

This was not looking good. An uneasy chill slithered down his spine. "Care to explain?"

"It doesn't matter now."

It was inconceivable that she would go back to Chavez. Just the thought turned his blood cold. "Fallon?"

For a brief moment she appeared lost in thought. When she looked at him her expression was bleak. The air of surrender enveloped her. "I made a promise that Chavez would die before I joined Christy. I failed her, again."

He didn't like the desolate ring to her voice or what she was implying. "Join Christy?"

"Adrian," pain washed across Fallon's face, "without her there isn't anything on Earth worth living for."

Her words hit him like a blow to the gut—or maybe it was his heart. She didn't feel the same about him as he did her. "Nothing, Fallon?" He hated the hurt that echoed in his ears.

Silence was her answer.

When she finally spoke, she murmured, "I promised Christy." Fallon glanced out the window longingly, then back at him. Gently, she cupped his face. On tiptoes, she brushed her mouth across his. "We have a couple hours before the sun rises and I have to go." Her lips thinned. "Make love to me."

She wouldn't really go through with her ridiculous oath—greet the morning—end her life?

Turmoil like he had never felt before rushed him, threatening to devour him. When had this woman become so important to him? Plans were already in place to ensure her safety. But there was nothing he could do to stop her from joining her daughter if she chose to.

Unexpected anger rose. His fingers closed firmly around her wrists. "What about us, Fallon?"

"Us?"

"You. Me." The urge to shake some sense into her built inside him. But he held his temper beneath the surface. His grip didn't tighten, but his voice did. "Isn't a life together worth living for?"

For a second he thought a flicker of affection, yearning shadowed her eyes, but it was quickly erased by a look of regret.

"I can't ask you to endanger your life as well as your people. I learned that with the battle you fought with Dominic. Chavez will find me, especially if I stay here. Running is the only chance I have." The tendons in her throat grew taut. "I'm tired of running. And I won't live under his control. I have no choice."

Adrian released her, moving one hand beneath her silky hair and cupping the nape of her neck. "Do you trust me?"

"Yes," she whispered.

"Then leave your safety in my hands." He guided her forward, so that their naked bodies came together, hers soft against his firmness.

As he leaned in to capture her mouth, she said, "Adrian, this is my fight—not yours."

He felt her breath warm against his face. "It became mine the minute we exchanged blood. I made that choice—me—not you. I knew the consequences and now your battle is mine." Then he closed the distance between them.

Adrian's kiss was tender, heartfelt, as he gently slid his tongue along the seam of her mouth, coaxing her to open to him and surrender. Her lips parted and his tongue slipped past them as easily as the man had invaded her heart.

Too much had happened, too soon.

The caress ended, but his lips continued a path of soft affection down her throat making her knees wobbly. She was emotionally drained and what little energy was left he stole. Her head lolled back, loving the way he forcefully held her, while at the same time touching her as if she were a priceless piece of glass that might shatter.

What he offered Fallon she had only dreamed about—freedom from tyranny and sweet revenge.

"So soft," he murmured.

In a slow, sensual touch his other hand caressed where her spine curved into her ass, wedging his finger between the rounded globes. Silent heat brushed across her skin as she felt the tenderness in her ass disappear with just a thought from Adrian.

But what would be the cost if she took him up on his offer to protect her? Fallon had nothing to lose and everything to gain. After Chavez was gone she would join Christy.

But what about Adrian?

Were his feelings for her fleeting infatuation? At times she could almost swear that he cared for her, like now as he stroked her body into a slow, simmering burn. And what if he did care? It wasn't morally right to play with his affections.

"Relax, darlin'. Let me pleasure you." His voice was husky, sexy as his tongue teased the pulse in her neck.

His arousal stirred. She felt it hard against her belly, and heard it in the increase of his pulse as his blood surged through his veins awakening her hunger. The ache in her gums throbbed. Her own desire tightened low in her belly. Her nipples grew sensitive against his chest.

It seemed silly, but in two short days she had come to care for him—maybe, too much. It didn't make sense.

Yeah. She'd heard of love at first sight, but the idea was a romantic fantasy. Things like that didn't happen to *real* people. Very few humans were gifted with a happily ever after. Why would an immortal be blessed with something or someone so precious?

She gasped as his fingertips pushed between their bodies and through the nest of hair at the apex of her thighs. With his foot he wedged her feet apart. But he didn't caress the area that became damp with just the thought of his touch.

It was becoming more difficult to think. All she really wanted was to love this man. Feel him deep inside her body driving away all the ugliness in her life.

"Quit thinking so hard," he whispered next to her ear. Then he whisked her into his arms and carried her to the bed. Gently, he laid her upon the comforter. The bed moaned beneath his weight as he crawled beside her and pulled her against his chest. "Let me chase your nightmares away."

He rolled her softly onto her back, parted her thighs and slipped between them. With one thrust he entered her. His eyes were warm and caring as he moved in and out of her body.

"Stay with me, Fallon," he murmured. The longing in his voice squeezed her heart.

She palmed the taut muscles in his arms from his wrist to his shoulders and back again. He was strength personified. And he felt so good buried deep inside her.

The tension low in her belly grew tighter and tighter, as did her grasp on his arms. With an arch of her back she was bathed in the heat of her climax. It wasn't an earth shattering release, but calm—almost serene, the tender moment endearing as she heard Adrian groan and join her.

After the pulse died, he leaned in, his weight pinning her to the bed as he slanted his mouth across hers. Again, his kiss was tender. He feathered soft affection along her neck, before he drifted to his side and pulled her to him.

In the quiet of the night he held her.

Fallon woke to the sensation of something between her thighs. A single finger parted her folds as Adrian stroked the inside of her labia with long, slow passes.

"I must have fallen asleep." She was wet, his movements slick and easy as another finger filled her. The glide of her hips against his hand increased. Friction and heat built rapidly inside her with his expert touch.

"Uh, huh. But you need to feed and it's too early to go aground." He bent and took her nipple into his mouth. The suction against her breast sent shards of sensations straight to her core.

"Adrian, I need you inside me." She felt desperate to feel him, desperate to cling to everything he offered—a future and more.

His mouth twitched with male pride. "What do you want, darlin'?" A hint of laughter took the edge off of his seductive question.

God, he was beautiful.

"Are you going to make me ask?" Her eyelids felt heavy, as they slid half-mast. She parted her mouth on a deep breath, as his finger played with her clit.

A devilish gleam lit his eyes, as he shook his head. "No…" he paused for a sinful second, "I'm gonna make you beg."

"Never," she laughed. God, she needed to laugh. It felt so good. And she loved the playful mood he was in. It was hard to stay trapped in despair when he offered her a moment of pure bliss, a moment to forget what awaited her. And she would take what he willingly offered.

"Never?" His brow rose with the challenge. He chuckled, and she felt his cock jerk against her hip. "What if I asked you to prop your leg on that chair by the window, so that I could taste the honey between your thighs?"

Her mouth curved faintly. "I'd do it, but it wouldn't affect me." Just the anticipation of what he proposed raised her pulse. It didn't help that he took that moment to bury his finger deep inside her.

His smile was slow and knowing, as his finger pushed in and out of her pussy. "No?"

She shrugged as if indifferent. "No."

He glanced quickly around the bedroom. "Then would I be correct that if I dragged that same chair in front of the standing mirror over there by the closet door, had you place your palms on the seat and watch me as I fucked you from behind…you wouldn't be affected?"

Well, dammit. The heavy flow of her juices against his steadily moving hand was a dead giveaway that the last suggestion had definite potential in breaking her will.

"Not at all." The catch in her throat was probably not very convincing. Nor was the way her thighs wedged further apart, so that he had better access to her swollen folds.

His smile widened, as his eyes darkened into molten gold. "Liar." He slid his hand deeper between her legs, his finger grazing the tight entrance of her anus. "What if I took you here?"

The pressure exerted against her rosebud made her gasp and a shiver to whisper up her spine.

Oh, yeah. That would do it. Still she remained aloof. "Been there— Done that—"

Crap. This game was getting more difficult by the second. Small spasms exploded in her pussy. She was unbelievably wet and beyond horny. Even still, there was something special in their play. Something she had never before experienced in such a sexual scenario.

His hand disappeared from between her thighs, moving over her hip, tucking beneath her ass to slip along the cleft, until he once again reached her tight entrance.

When his finger eased inside, stretching and filling her, Fallon couldn't stop his name from touching her lips. "*Adrian.*" Sweet pain exploded inside her taut opening, but didn't last long.

Compliments of Adrian's magic, the chair next to the window suddenly moved, scraping across the floor in its haste and coming to a stop before the mirror.

Anticipation tightened low in her belly. Fireworks went off just below the surface in each nipple.

Another finger joined the first, spreading her further. The fiery sensation made her groan aloud.

He looked at her with stark, hot eyes. "Tell me what you want, darlin'."

"You," she said breathlessly.

If only she meant it, but he knew they both were walking a tightrope. No matter her choice he wanted to make their time together special and fun. Help her forget the tragedy in her life and show her there was still something to live for.

Adrian removed his fingers from her body, cleansing them with a thought as he rolled off the bed, taking her with him. With determined steps, he guided her backward in front of the mirror.

"You should see what I see." He was so aroused that his balls felt rock-hard, sensitive against his thighs. Every movement sent rays of fire throughout his groin. He couldn't wait to take her. Nevertheless, he sucked in a breath, forcing himself to move slowly as he positioned her so the length of her right side showed in the looking glass.

"Look at yourself. You're so beautiful," he murmured, before he cupped her breasts, feeling the weight in his palms.

It was true. In her aroused state her skin flushed a light shade of pink. Her gorgeous hair draped her shoulders, and her violet eyes darkened with desire. Breasts rounded and full, her nipples were rosy peaks. A tiny waist flared out at hips that led to shapely legs.

Damn. It ratcheted his lust up further as she watched him in the mirror.

But it was her backside that now had his attention, as he stepped back and took an appreciative look. His gaze traveled down the curve of her back over her firm ass. That particular part of her body was simply delicious and offered a special treat this night.

"Palms on the chair. Keep your eyes on the mirror." A shiver raced across his heated flesh. Just the thought of fucking her ass made his body tense.

She followed his directions obediently.

When he stood behind her he slipped a foot between hers and pried them further apart. Bent over and spread wide for him, the submissive position was a rush to his groin.

"Mine," he growled. He grasped her ass and squeezed each cheek with his palms. Then he spread them apart, staring at the puckered skin where he would soon bury his cock.

Fallon whimpered, "Adrian, don't make me wait."

For a moment he stared at her, exposed and awaiting him. Did she have any idea what the knowledge did to him? Something fluttered in his chest and for a moment he thought he was having a heart attack. Of course, it was impossible. He was already dead, but by the way his body burned inside he wouldn't swear to it.

"Adrian?" Fallon whimpered.

She needed to be fucked. He could see desire in her eyes, as he prepared her for his invasion. Her intense gaze followed him to the nightstand next to the bed, where he opened the drawer and removed a tube of lubricant. He unscrewed the top, squeezing plenty of the contents upon two fingers. With a twist he tightened the lid back, laid the container on the tabletop, and then approached her. When he spread the clear substance at her entrance, his finger pressing deep inside her, she gasped. After he had worked the gel thoroughly in and around the tender area his second finger joined the first.

"*Ahhh…*" she purred, so soft and sweetly. " More."

He answered by cleansing his fingers and taking himself in hand, before he positioned his cock at her rosebud and slowly nudged the entrance, driving past the first tight ring. Then he grasped her hips and gave her another inch of his rigid erection. Slowly easing forward, adding another inch, and another—until he was seated deep inside her.

Talk about hot and tight. This had to be heaven, with Fallon being his angel.

With a slight backward lean, his gaze fixated on his cock moving in and out, stretching the taut orifice. He sucked a strangled breath between clenched teeth. "Damn woman." He ground his hips against her, and then rotated them.

Her body jerked. Her elbows bent and almost gave out, before she straightened them. "Oh, God." Her heated cry was a turn on as her fangs burst from her gums. Blood tinted the incisors. The copper smell woke the beast in him and called upon his canines to drop.

With one hand he reached for a handful of her hair, pulling back so that her neck arched gently. The other hand he caressed to the nest of curls at the vee of her thighs. He found her swollen nub and circled it several times.

"Ssss…" She hissed, baring her fangs. Hunger and need raged in the depths of her eyes.

"Yeah, darlin'." He thrust back and forth, harder and faster. "Feel the burn." He thrust his finger deep inside her pussy.

The reflection in the mirror was the embodiment of an erotic fantasy.

Wild and primitive.

Their species dated back to the dawn of time. Vampires were sensual in nature, but he had never imagined reaching the heights of ecstasy that this woman had carried him to. She brought out the need in him to protect what was his—and Fallon was his.

He held his breath, fighting the oncoming orgasm, needing to prolong the vision in the mirror, as well as the intense sensation whipping through him. His balls tightened painfully against his body as he gulped down a mouthful of air. Just as he felt the force rush through his cock, releasing in a fiery stream, Fallon screamed.

Gaze pinned to their reflections, he slammed his hips against her ass and stopped. He couldn't move nor breathe as his climax rocketed through him.

With several quick, twitchy movements her vaginal muscles tightened around his finger. A low, gratifying groan flowed from her parted lips. She jerked, arching her back and raising her head. He listened to the sounds of her sharp gasps, once—twice, and then she released another sated groan.

The peaceful expression on her face matched his as he withdrew from her body, cleansing them both with just a thought.

She straightened, stretching her arms high above her. He heard the contentment in her sigh falter as her brows furrowed. Her arms drifted to her side. She turned to face him.

"Adrian, we need to talk—"

He placed a finger against her lips. "Come to bed with me. Wake in my arms." Now it was his turn to beg, because if that's what it took, by damn he'd do it. There was no way he would allow Fallon to simply walk out of his life or throw her life away.

Indecision played across her face. With a single nod she surrendered.

A sense of relief engulfed him, releasing in one gush the breath he didn't know he had held. He pulled her into his embrace, his chin resting on the top of her head.

He had won—at least for another day.

Chapter Fourteen

Uneasiness slithered beneath her skin when Fallon stepped outside the house. A cold rush of anxiety smacked her in the face as her boots touched the ground. Men and women, human and vampire, ran aimlessly across the yard. Some barked orders, while close by she heard a woman sobbing like her heart would break. Tension hung heavy in the night air. Even the dark clouded sky looked angry. The deep resonant sound of thunder seemed to echo something was wrong—dead wrong.

When Fallon had awakened to find herself alone she should have known all was not well. The silence of the house as she strolled through it was another sign. Even the kitchen where Sally usually stood kneading dough for the following days' meals was empty.

The first thing that came to Fallon's mind was Maggie. All men had somewhat of a pack mentality with an alpha on top. Had one of her ex-Master's minions stepped into his shoes and felt the woman belonged to him? Was she missing? Okay?

Before Fallon allowed her imagination to soar, she reached out and stopped Doreen with an outstretched hand. "What's going on?"

"Billy—Susan and George's son is missing."

"Missing?"

The blonde jerked from Fallon's grasp, running past her into the house. But not before she speared Fallon with an incriminating look that was hot enough to ignite into flames the jeans and red, short-sleeve T-shirt Fallon wore.

A sour and bitter taste clawed up her throat. She fought the nausea and dizziness. As her knees buckled, she gripped the hitching post next to her, bracing herself from a sure fall. The wood was cool and rough as she clung to it to steady herself.

Chavez.

Like a sieve she felt life flow from her body. *Another child*— She couldn't finish her thought. It couldn't be happening again. Had her selfishness to hold onto Adrian for one more night brought more evil upon Adrian's people?

From the corner of the house Sally appeared. Her arm draped around her crying daughter's shoulders. As they grew closer, the woman's sobs were a knife cutting straight to Fallon's heart. She knew the deep wrenching emptiness Susan was feeling—knew the desperation to have her child in her arms once again.

"Sally," Fallon said as the woman's red puffy eyes met hers. "Is there anything I can do?"

Doreen exited the house holding an armful of flashlights as she came to a stop. With a toss of her head her long mane flowed over one shoulder. She huffed, "Haven't you done enough?" The venom in her words was nothing compared to the accusation in her voice. She shook her head in disgust, and then continued on to cross the yard coming upon a group of men who reached for the flashlights.

"Never mind her. Billy was Doreen's favorite." Amazingly, Sally's tone held no accusation.

"How long has he been gone?" Fallon hoped this was just a false alarm, that they'd find the little three year old hiding or playing with his older siblings.

"Susan bathed Billy around seven o'clock. He was tired so she put him to bed. When she went in to check on him an hour later, he was gone." Fresh tears rose in Sally's eyes as she patted Susan lightly on the arm. "Let's go inside, dear."

Susan jerked to a stop as if her feet became rooted. "No." Panic twisted her features as she quickly scanned the yard. A wild, almost crazed expression replaced the one of panic. "I have to look for Billy. *BILLY…*" she yelled, fighting her mother's hold as she tried to get away. All the while her sobs became louder, more strangled, a mixture of pain and anger.

A feeling Fallon knew all too well.

Susan pulled out of Sally's grip as soon as she saw George approach from the barn. His brawny arms opened and wrapped around Susan. "Baby, don't cry. Me and the boys, we'll find the little devil." His chuckle fell flat, as well as his heartfelt attempt to assure his wife. "Shhh… Baby, *please* don't cry." The mournful whine in the big man's voice nearly brought Fallon to her knees.

With the grace of God, Fallon held onto her composure by a mere thread. Hot, angry emotion stung her eyes. "I'll find him."

George's smile was as weak as his chuckle had been. "Thank you. But the men folk are searching. Best you stay here with Susan and her ma." He angled his head to gain Susan's attention. "Baby, I need to go now. I'll bring our boy back home."

Susan covered her mouth with her hand, forcing back the cries that refused to stop. She nodded rapidly, allowing her mother to embrace her once again and guide her into the house.

Silently, George stood for a moment and watched his wife disappear in the house. When he knew she was safely inside he tipped his hat to Fallon and walked away. Some distance between them he stopped in the shadow of a large pine tree. Fallow saw his shoulders begin to quake, saw the stream of tears racing down his cheeks. He hung his head, swiping away the evidence of his heart breaking with the back of his hand. With a deep, shuddering breath he continued onward.

Fallon pushed away from the hitching post. She couldn't just stand around and wait for Chavez. If he had Billy maybe she could talk him into letting the child go. Fat chance. But what else did she have? She gazed around at the mountainous land stretching in all directions.

"Where do you think you're going?"

She glanced over her shoulder to see Adrian heading straight for her. She was hell-bent that he wouldn't stop her. "I'm going to search for Billy." She increased her steps.

"No, you're not." With long, determined strides he easily caught up with her. A hand on her biceps brought her to a stop. Gently he pressed his lips to her forehead.

She angled her chin staring up at him. "Yes. I am."

Lightning raced across the sky sending shadows across Adrian's face as it hardened. "No."

She breathed in the fresh scent of the upcoming storm. "Yes."

"Damn it, Fallon, don't argue with me on this one." Thunder cracked with the same intensity in his tone.

"It's Chavez. I know he has the boy."

"You don't know that." He ran his palms up and down her arms. "We'll find him."

"And you don't know that it isn't Chavez." She felt raindrops fall, but only a few, as if it were a mere warning.

"I'm sure of it."

Liar. He was only attempting to reassure her. "Then it won't hurt for me to join the search party."

"No," he answered sharply. "I want you in the house. Safe."

"So, you think it might be Chavez, too?"

He jerked off his hat and ran his fingers through his mused hair. "Darlin', I just can't take the chance you might be right."

"He wants me."

Menace vibrated from Adrian's throat. "Over my dead body." He placed his hat squarely on his head.

"Be reasonable."

"Reasonable? I thought I was being reasonable."

"You can't make me stay here." Fallon couldn't fathom being the cause of the child's abduction. Adrian couldn't expect her to remain behind, to sit across the table from people who might blame her for the missing boy.

Adrian must have sensed her discomfort. "Dammit. You can come with me, but you *must* follow my instructions to the t."

"Yes, sir."

"Don't test me, Fallon," he warned. "I'll do whatever is necessary to ensure your safety. Now, c'mon and stay close."

With a rise of his hand he masked both of them from human sight. Fallon heard Adrian's bones and tendons pop—shifting. It was a beautiful sight to see soft, downy feathers bud from his pores, covering his body, as his arms shifted into large, extended wings that spanned at least eight feet wide. As his facial features melted into sharp eyes and a beak, his legs morphed, his feet becoming strong talons. He raised his beak toward the sky and released a cry that echoed in the night.

And then he was airborne. A beautiful wingspan against the dark sky, she knew he masked his actual size from human eyes. They would see only what he wanted them to see, a normal raven.

As Fallon began to shift into mist, he spoke to her telepathically, *"Take the form of a bird. I can keep a better eye on you."*

"I can't." It was humiliating to admit her inabilities. But she had never possessed the strength to morph into an animal of any sort. The best she could do was fur, maybe a tail or pointed ears.

In a large circle, he soared high above her head. *"Hold an image of a bird in your mind and the rest will come."*

Frustration drove her fists to her hips. "I didn't say I didn't know how—I said I can't." They were wasting precious time arguing.

"I don't want to hear I can't. Try." Impatience clung on each of his words.

"Well, shit," she huffed. Reasoning with him was like rationalizing with a brick wall. She dragged a deep breath into her lungs. Might as well get it over with and prove her point.

Fallon closed her eyes and envisioned a large Gyrfalcon with white plumage and black barring on its back and wings. She had once read a story to Christy of the large, majestic bird.

All of a sudden a tingle spread across her skin, tiny pinpricks of sensation that made her nerve endings stand on end. Like easing into a soft coat, she opened her eyes to see her body covered in white down. Bones and tendons made grinding, popping sounds as she extended her arms and watched beautiful flight feathers jut out. She wasn't extremely impressed with the tough-hide of her legs, but her talons and curved beak were sharp.

A high-pitched shrill was her cry of joy. "*I did it.*" She spread her wings wide, and then lunged into the sky.

"*Of course you did, but an eagle would have been more functional. An Artic bird?*" He laughed.

"*Yeah, but aren't I pretty? And much larger than the real thing.*" She flapped her wings, climbing higher into the sky.

What a thrill. Fallon couldn't believe the way the wind stroked and lifted her feathers. Caught in her moment of triumph she almost forgot what sent them into the air. "*Where should we begin searching?*"

"*The others are searching the more populated places closer by. It's strange that I haven't been able to sense him.*"

"*Like Maggie?*"

"*This is different. I wasn't prepared for Dominic—I am prepared for Chavez. But something's off. I can't quite put my finger on it. I don't sense danger. Yet we searched the house and property. Billy just isn't there.*"

Fallon wanted desperately to believe him. But he was right. There was no evil lingering in the air, no disturbance in the land.

Together they soared over mountaintops, dipped close to ground in wooded areas so that their keen eyesight could search between the trees. They passed stream after stream of running water and several small lakes.

But there was no sign of Billy.

If Adrian didn't suspect foul play why were they searching so far away from the house? A small boy could never wander off this distance in the time he'd been missing.

A few raindrops fell, but they beaded and rolled off her wings, as she easily soared through the air.

From high above the ground, Fallon noticed that the green lushness of the scenery began to change. Below her the land appeared scorched, damaged, as if a wildfire had touched it. She hated the painful vibes the earth gave off.

"*Isn't this where you fought the battle with that Master vampire?*"

"*Yes,*" Adrian responded dryly.

She could feel the lingering depravity that Dominic had left behind as she swooped lower to take a look.

"*Look! Over there.*" In a shallow furrow Billy's little body lay in the fetal position. "*Is he alive?*" Fallon made a nosedive toward him.

"*Wait!*" Adrian's warning gave her pause and she halted mid-air pulling up. "*Stay behind me.*" They made three circles above the boy, each time the circle was smaller and each time they grew closer. "*I don't sense a trap, but the land is still crying from the previous battle. It's hard to hear and smell over its sorrow.*"

And that was the reason Adrian hadn't detected the child. The utterance of the injured land surrounding him and the grief it gave off for the boy's loss were blending together, confusing Adrian. Unlike with the child's parents he hadn't exchanged blood with the boy, allowing a personal link to be established.

As Adrian grew nearer relief washed over him. The gentle swish of Billy's heartbeat, slow and relaxed in sleep, assured him the child was alive. But how did he get here? It was too far for a three year old to travel within the hour he'd been gone.

With a keen eye he scanned the land and horizon prepared for anything, but strangely he still received no vibes that anything was amiss.

"Stay airborne. I'll retrieve Billy." In a graceful swoop Adrian caught Billy in his talons. At the same time he sent a command for the boy to remain asleep. It would do neither of them any good if Billy woke during the flight home. Adrian touched the boy's memories of the event. They had been wiped clean, leaving no trace as to who had done this to him. Additionally, there had been a veil erected to keep predators away as he lay in his little trench.

It didn't make sense. This was not done by Chavez. Adrian was positive that he would have known if Chavez invaded his territory. So who was to blame for Billy's abduction?

With the boy held close to his chest, Adrian rose into the sky to join Fallon. A brush of her wing as she flew by stroked the boy's dark hair back out of his eyes. *"Poor thing. He must have been so frightened."*

Adrian didn't share his concerns with her as they tried to beat the storm.

Within the cover of some pine trees Fallon and Adrian landed and quickly shape-shifted back into their human form. Billy whimpered in Adrian's arms and he drew him closer as he released the hold he had on the child's mind.

"It's raining," Billy grumbled, blinking back the drops that hit upon his eyes. "Ma's gonna be mad if I get wet."

Adrian shared a smile with Fallon. "I have a feeling your mother is going to be so happy to see you she'll let you play in the storm."

"Really?" His little voice rose with excitement.

"Don't count on it," Fallon cautioned.

The minute they came into the floodlights of the yard they were bombarded with people. Cougar moved his hand quickly over the top of the boy's head.

"Hey." Billy tossed the man a frown.

The noise must have alerted Susan because she flew out the backdoor, Sally hot behind her, skirts flowing around her legs. George came around the corner in a full run arriving beside Adrian at the same time Susan did. The woman was still crying, but this time for joy.

George ripped the child from Adrian's arms and held him so tightly, Billy groaned, "Daddy, I can't breathe." George's laughter was a mixture of relief and happiness, as he wrapped his arm around his wife.

As the rain started to fall, Adrian said, "Perhaps you should take the rascal into the house."

"But you said Ma would let me play in the rain," Billy argued, sitting up in his father's brawny arms.

Adrian grimaced. Fallon snickered.

"He did, did he?" Susan's attempt to sound gruff just didn't work. "I think Adrian was mistaken."

George slipped Billy into Susan's waiting arms, but not before he kissed the boy soundly on the forehead. "Take him in the house. I need to talk to the boss." When his family was out of earshot, he turned to Adrian. "Well?"

Adrian had full intentions on briefing his people, but didn't wish to worry Fallon further. He ignored George and instead turned to Fallon. "You're getting wet. Why don't you go inside?"

She shot him a quick, assessing look. "You wouldn't be trying to get rid of me would you?"

"Never," he lied, but he knew she saw through it. "With all the commotion I haven't checked on Maggie. Would you do it for me?"

"Dammit, Adrian. If this is about Chavez I have a right to know."

Adrian didn't have time to argue with her. "You and I both know if this was Chavez's work Billy wouldn't be alive." Fallon flinched, but didn't say another word. "Now, please go check on Maggie. You and I'll talk later."

She wasn't happy. But evidently she felt he spoke the truth as she turned and walked away.

"So?" George moved before him.

Adrian explained what little he knew about the abduction finishing with, "Looks like we have another threat from an unknown source."

Chapter Fifteen

As Fallon approached Maggie's bedroom door the woman inside snapped, "No. I won't." Behind the hard oak door she heard Tucker's voice. "C'mon, Maggie. You have to feed."

"Not from you." Maggie's annoyance rose in tone.

Lightly, Fallon tapped on the door.

Maggie said, "Come in," as Tucker replied at the same time, "Go away."

Before Fallon stepped inside the room, she called to Adrian using their mental link. "*Adrian. The children are fighting. Maggie's hunger is driving Tucker wild.*"

"*I'll be there as soon as I can. Keep them apart.*"

"*Yeah. Right.*"

From the fire in Tucker's eyes that matched the color of Maggie's flaming hair, Fallon would be lucky if he didn't toss her out on her ass. He paced the floor, glaring at both she and Maggie, before he sat in the chair by the bed. Maggie lay propped against several pillows with a blanket pulled to her waist. A silky black nightgown showed above the bunched bedding.

A smile touched Fallon's lips. "How are you doing tonight?"

Maggie flashed an agitated glance in Tucker's direction. "I'd be a lot better if he wasn't here." Her features softened. "Did they find Billy?"

"Yes. He's safe and sound with Susan."

Concern creased Maggie's forehead. "Does Adrian know what happened?"

"Don't bother yourself with that," Tucker barked. "Adrian will take care of everything."

Fallon wasn't sure whether there was a hint of sarcasm in Tucker's words or if the man was in a rather bad mood.

"I didn't ask your opinion," Maggie snapped, then pinned him with a hot glare.

"Dammit, Maggie." He pushed from the chair and stomped across the room. With his arms folded tight across his chest, he leaned against the wall and watched her like a predator.

Okay. So Tucker was in a bad mood.

Maggie rolled her eyes toward the ceiling. "I need to get out of this room."

"You're not going anywhere," Tucker barked, stepping away from the wall. "You are the most unreasonable woman I've ever met."

Tucker was right in this case that she shouldn't go anywhere. Even Fallon could sense that some of Maggie's internal wounds had not healed as fast as any of them had expected. Fallon shivered with what Dominic had done to Maggie before Adrian got to her.

"Maggie, Tucker's right. You really should be resting aground. And you need to feed. Adrian will be here shortly."

"She wouldn't be hungry, if she'd let me take care of her needs." Tucker pinched the bridge of his nose as if he fought to constrain his temper. When he looked up again, he appeared weary. "Baby, let me hold you—feed you."

Maggie's lips thinned. "No" was her answer, but her eyes said differently. A blind man could see she loved Tucker, and apparently he loved her. He hadn't left her side since the attack. So why was it so difficult for the two of them to lay down the barbs and kiss and make up?

Fallon didn't get time to ponder the thought before the door opened and Adrian waltzed in.

His smile was genuine as he strolled to the side of the bed and sat down. "How's my patient today?" He cupped her hand in his.

"I'm perfectly fine, Adrian. Will you dismiss your guard dog now?"

He glanced toward Tucker and back to Maggie. "How about I make you a deal? You go aground and let your wounds heal properly. We'll see how you feel when you rise."

Fallon didn't understand why Maggie hadn't gone aground after the first night. Vampires healed faster with the assistance of the elements. The land held special properties, rich in natural minerals.

"No," Maggie said.

Tucker crossed the room and stood over her. "Baby, you have to." There was an ache in his voice as he conceded. "I won't bother you anymore." He pivoted, heading toward the door. Fingers closed around the doorknob, he paused. For a moment Fallon thought he'd turn around, instead he opened the door then closed it softly behind him.

Maggie's eyes misted.

Adrian squeezed Maggie's hand. "You two can't go on like this."

Maggie blinked away the telltale emotion. With a lift of her chin, she raised a single brow. "I don't know what you're talking about."

"Fine." Adrian undid the button at his cuff and pushed up his sleeve, before he extended Maggie his wrist. "Feed."

She gripped Adrian's arm, accepting what he offered. As she drank, color touched her cheeks. No one spoke as Maggie fed.

With a swipe of her tongue across the wound she released his arm and sank back into the pillows. A heavy sigh pushed from her lungs.

Adrian rose. "Go aground now. I'll secure your resting place so that you will not be bothered."

She nodded. "Thank you for understanding."

"Sleep well." Adrian gathered Fallon's hand in his and led her out of the room. Quietly, he shut the door behind them.

"Understanding what?" Fallon asked.

"Tucker refuses to sleep apart from Maggie, so she refuses to go aground."

With a quick move, Adrian pinned Fallon against the wall and took her mouth in a hungry kiss.

His mouth was fierce, hot and ruthless. Heat came off his body in waves.

Unease slithered across her skin. She placed her palms on his board, solid chest and gave him a little push. "What's wrong?"

"Nothing." He pressed his forehead to hers. "Everything."

She wrapped her arms around his waist. "Talk to me, Adrian."

"Tucker and Maggie are really screwing up." His head rose slightly as he locked his gaze to hers. "I don't want to make the same mistake."

Fallon didn't know what to say, so she remained quiet.

His knuckles lightly grazed her cheek. "I'll make you a deal." His warm breath brushed her face.

"Seems to be the night for making deals." Her attempt to melt the tension building beneath his touch failed.

He inhaled deeply. "This might not be the time or place, but here's the deal. I want you." The truth sparked in his eyes. His hands moved down her arms, fingers circling her wrists. His body pressed tightly to hers. Then he jerked his hands to her face to cup her cheeks and looked deeply into her eyes. "Not for tonight or tomorrow—but forever."

Forever? Fallon felt her eyes widen.

A knee wedged between her legs brought him even closer. He was fully aroused his cock hard against her belly. He wrapped his arms around her waist, pulling her nearer.

"Stay," he whispered against her mouth. This time his kiss was tender and sweet.

Emotion rose quickly only to crash and burn somewhere in her throat when the kiss ended. How ironic was it that she found a man who wanted a future when none existed for her?

His expression hardened. "Chavez will never touch you again. In exchange for my protection promise you'll stay with me—forever."

Fallon didn't have forever. Still she'd be an idiot to pass up what Adrian offered.

Acid churned in her stomach as she prepared herself to deceive Adrian. But she couldn't do it, not staring directly into his warm eyes. Instead she closed her eyes and murmured, "Yes," before she pressed her lips to his.

She felt the joy in his tight embrace. It nearly tore her apart.

Dammit! Wasn't revenge supposed to be sweet? Shouldn't she be happy to be joining Christy? If so, then why did it feel like her heart was breaking?

Tears touched her eyes.

"Happy tears?" he asked, brushing them away with a finger.

"Yes." Another lie.

Fallon wasn't fooling Adrian.

She wore her lie beneath a clear veneer. It hurt, but he would never let her see his pain. Call him a fool, but he knew the bond between them was more than a flighty notion. In time perhaps she would grow to care for him. Now if only Chavez would stay out of the picture long enough for him to persuade Fallon that they belonged together.

What was it about this woman that broke down all his defenses?

Mine.

"Adrian." A hint of alarm rose in her voice. "Too tight," she squeezed out airily.

Chagrined, he released the taut grip he had on her and took a step backward. "Sorry."

"It's okay. Is something wrong?"

"No." Now it was his turn to lie. "I need to hunt. Neither of us has fed since we rose. Maggie took what reserve I had." Billy's disappearance had taken priority to everything, even feeding. "Fly with me." He took her hand and headed down the hall.

Her face brightened. "I still can't believe that I made the conversion. It was so cool. As mist I feel tossed around a lot." He heard her excitement as they entered the living room. The house was quiet.

Thank God, Billy was home and okay.

"Darlin', I have a lot to teach you." He wanted to teach her everything.

The front door squeaked as he pulled it open and let her pass through. Rain had dampened the ground. The clean scent mingled with the smell of the soil around him.

With Chavez bringing Fallon into the world of immortality, Adrian doubted that she had the opportunity to appreciate the gifts she had been given. It was true that so much was taken from her. Still if she could find an ounce of happiness she would see that life could be beautiful. Adrian wanted to be the man who opened that door for Fallon.

Her smile deepened. "You'll teach me more?"

"Sure." The most important thing she needed to learn was how to protect herself against an enemy. In a struggle with a Master vampire she would be nearly helpless, but there were some things she could do to baffle him, hopefully allowing her enough time to get away.

Fallon had taken the first step by ensuring that she fed properly. Even to a vampire proper nutrition was important. He could feel her getting stronger. He doubted she even knew the strength she possessed now that his blood ran through her veins.

Adrian had no intentions of allowing Chavez to get within reach of Fallon, but there were still things that would help her in awkward situations, illusion being one of them. People tended to see and believe what they wanted. The hunted had to use knowledge and intelligence to their advantage.

"We'll feed and then your training begins."

Within seconds they were airborne.

They hadn't gone but a short distance when Adrian spied a campground. The smell of burning pine rose as the couple sat around the campfire chatting.

Fallon, in Gyrfalcon form, landed beside a large blue spruce. He felt her eyes watching as he took human form and approached the campsite.

The young man of medium build rose, placing himself between Adrian and the woman who got to her feet. "Can I help you?"

A quick mind scan and Adrian discovered the couple was married. Their names were Paul and Maria Sweet. As he touched their memories he saw their recent wedding, and the child growing in Maria's belly she had yet to tell her husband about. He sensed her excitement, subdued by worry. Would her husband share her joy?

Adrian wasted no time bewitching them, muddling their thoughts so that he could feed. Maria waited patiently for her turn, while Paul came willingly into Adrian's arms. The man was strong and virile, angling his head to allow Adrian access to the vein that pulsed at his throat. Adrian wasted no time. His fangs sank deep into the man's tender skin.

Careful to take only what he needed, Adrian assisted Paul to sit. With a charming smile on Maria's face she stepped forward.

The shrill squawk sent a rush through Adrian. His little bird had sensed Maria's condition. He hadn't planned to take the woman's blood, not now that he knew she carried a life.

"Maria, take care of your man. He's feeling a little weak." As she turned to obey, Adrian shape-shifted, taking flight to join Fallon who had lifted into the air.

Luckily not far down the road there were two men sleeping within their tent. Their loud intermingling snores revealed they slept deeply. "I won't be long," Adrian said.

His bird form made a beeline for the green canvas. Adrian changed shape just before he landed softly on the ground. With a swipe of his hand the flap opened and he disappeared inside.

Minutes later he stepped from the shelter—sated. It was time for Fallon's first lesson.

Chapter Sixteen

So damn sexy. Fallon's heart did a little flip-flop. Adrian leaned with his back against a large pine tree just outside the campgrounds at Reservation Lake where he had fed. With his cowboy hat pulled low to shadow his eyes it gave him a dark, mysterious quality. A single knee bent, the sole of one boot pressed to the bark, tightened the material across his crotch. The allure he presented beneath the moonlight nearly drove her to distraction.

His mouth twitched into a sexy grin. He straightened and crooked a finger to beckon her to his side. "Hungry?"

"Starving." She moved into his open arms. His warm embrace made her heart flutter. The light sensation shot down her body, reappearing low in her belly. With a shift of her feet she snuggled closer, smelling the raw masculine scent that was uniquely Adrian's. Amazingly, she felt safe and something more—cherished. He didn't attempt to hide his feelings as he opened his thoughts to her. He genuinely cared about her.

Men like the one who held her just didn't really exist, did they? "Too good to be true" crossed her mind. But the feel of his hands in her hair as he drew her nearer proved he was real. The magical way he stole her breath with a kiss confirmed just how good he was.

"Darlin', you drive me wild." His deep, sensual voice, and the fact his hands were now palming her breasts through her red T-shirt, made her whimper with need. "I love the little sounds you make." He rubbed his nose against hers, his eyes pools of temptation. With a tilt of his head, he presented her with his neck.

The pressure of her canines dropping, pushing through gums and bone, made her mouth salivate. She couldn't help stroking the vein in his throat, teasing it with her tongue, before she bit down.

His low, grating groan was satisfying, even more so the presence of his hard cock against her hip. Light, tingling sensations rippled through her veins as she fed. She drank, loving the power that flowed from him to her like an invisible shield. It made her feel alive. Before she took too much, she smoothed her tongue over her bite marks. Her hands moved on their own accord slipping from around him and straight for his belt buckle. She needed to feel him between her thighs, thrusting deep inside her.

"Not now." He stilled her hands with his. "We have work to do. Then we'll play."

"Work?" She cupped his firm erection. "Are you sure?"

"Temptress." He chuckled, bringing her hands to his mouth and pressing a kiss to them. As he released her, his expression drew taut, an air of seriousness taking hold. "There're a couple of things I want to show you before the sun rises." He moved to a grouping of young trees as he spoke. "Control, as in illusion and deception, can be your friend."

When he said deception his voice lowered. She couldn't help wondering if the shadow drifting across his face was meant for her lies.

"Illusion can be used to plant a false idea or concept, allowing you to avoid a confrontation or possibly give you time to escape."

With his last word he disappeared, but she sensed he hadn't moved. The whisper of mist wasn't present. Then she saw the subtle movement in the sticky bark of the tree. She'd know those golden eyes anywhere.

"I didn't know we could do that."

He leaned forward. One minute he was one with the tree. The next he slowly visualized, turning from bark to flesh, before he stood in front of her. The sight was amazing.

"But what you want to do is confuse your target." He stepped back into the tree. But strangely the group of five trees each sported a pair of golden eyes. "You can duplicate yourself."

This time when he moved beyond the tree there were five of him in human form, each identical replicas of the man slowly stealing her heart. She sent fingers of detection to determine which image was real, but each of them she stroked felt as real as the next. Then, like a spring released, the five forms snapped together forming only one Adrian.

"Projecting yourself to be one place while you're somewhere else is invaluable in tricking your enemy. Plus it gives you time enough to flee."

"But how?"

"The secret is to leave a bit of your essence behind." He must have read her confusion, because he continued. "You mentioned earlier when you take the form of mist that sometimes you feel tossed about. You even experience the scattering of the drops, sort of like you're being torn asunder. In this case instead of gathering yourself together to form one mass, you leave behind a piece of yourself."

Fallon felt her eyes widen in disbelief.

"We regenerate quickly so there's no danger of not being able to materialize again. Of course you don't want to spread yourself too thinly. It will weaken you."

"Why is it that I could take the form of mist, but not a bird or cat?"

"Mist is water vapor with little mass, while a bird or cat is solid mass. You would never have had this problem if you had fed properly." The firmness in his tone was a reprimand. "You have wasted time in your growth as an immortal by rejecting what you have become."

Adrian remained quiet for a moment. He looked at her with assessing eyes. Then he stepped forward and cupped her face with his palms. "All things are created for a purpose, that includes what we are—vampires. Let me show you our world. A world that can be as wondrous as your previous life, but more sensual and seductive than any human could ever imagine."

The pull of temptation was almost inescapable. She wanted to surrender to his lure, if only for a second. But she could never forget the promise she'd made to Christy. Yet what stopped her from taking what he offered until it was time for her to say good-bye?

"Show me, Adrian."

He brushed his lips across hers and she felt his mouth curve into a satisfied smile. "I was hoping you'd say that. I know a place that is a little heaven here on Earth. But first I want you to practice what you've just learned."

Fallon thought of a fine mist. Shape-shifting, her body dissolved into tiny drops of dew. She hovered in the air awaiting his next direction.

"Now concentrate on each separate bead of moisture," Adrian coached as she felt the immediate feeling of disconnection, of being forced apart. "Push yourself in numerous directions toward several objects. They can be alive or inanimate. Then attach yourself to several of them."

Amazingly, she was able to adhere herself to several trees like Adrian had done. With another thought of wholeness, she drew her essence together and walked from the trees. A sense of pride bubbled up inside her, but it was nothing compared to his smile of approval.

"Good. Practice. You'll get better and faster with each time." He paused. "Come here." She stepped into his arms. His eyes grew dark. "Now let me show you my place."

He released her and once again they took the form of birds.

Adrian was majestic in any shape he chose. An impressive wing span swept up and down as if he moved without effort. Feathers darker than the night were highlighted against the gray clouds in the sky. And man could he shake those tail feathers, she thought, following him. She chuckled at her own joke. Her giggles turned into full body laughter.

"*What?*" he asked, soaring toward the ground and landing softly as he shape-shifted back into his human form.

As she joined him, she glanced at his backside. "Nice ass." It truly was a masterpiece wrapped in all that tight denim.

His smile was slow and sexy. "Come here."

Willingly, she went into his arms. He held her—nothing more— just held her like it was the most natural thing to do. Then he once again took her hand and led her down an embankment. With each step she had to bury her boots into the grass, pine needles and soil to make sure she didn't fall and roll down the mountainside.

In the distance she saw and heard a waterfall spilling into the mouth of the valley below where it continued to cut and zigzag through the land. The stream rushed over fallen trees and rocks.

Almost to the creek, Adrian stopped and sat down, pulling her with him. The slant of the hillside made it easy to lie on their backs and still see the stream, waterfall, and the rising mountain just beyond the water's edge.

"Reservation Lake is one of my favorite spots." He sighed, removed his hat and laid it beside him, before he slipped his hands behind his head.

"Hmmm…" She hummed with appreciation. It was peaceful and beautiful. In a place like this she could lose herself. Believe that the darkness that had surrounded her for over a year never existed and that the man beside her would always be there.

Downstream a whitetail deer cautiously approached the creek. Elegant and sleek, the doe's ears twitched, listening for danger. Slowly, she lowered her head, sipping from the cool water. Her big brown eyes looked so innocent.

Adrian was right about one thing. The night did hold a beauty. Her night vision as a vampire was sharp and clear.

"Adrian, how old are you?"

"Old," he chuckled.

"How'd it happen?"

He continued to stare at the stars. "I was thirty-three. Invincible."

Fallon was glad he gave no pretense of misunderstanding. She wanted to know how he became a vampire.

"I owned a fleet of ships that went from Newport, Rhode Island to the West Indies exporting plantation products like potatoes, vegetables, granite, and whatever else my ships could carry. Beautiful silks, spices and a variety of other exotic goods I brought home to sell and exchange. It was quite lucrative. I was on the top of the world financially. But—" He paused, adding, "I wanted more."

She couldn't read his blank expression as he looked blindly into the sky. A bird squawked in the distance. The water continued to whisper across the rocks.

"The sky warned of a storm. The tempest was swift in coming. Violent winds tore at our sails. Waves hundreds of feet in the air." He drew quiet. When he spoke again, his voice had softened. "Next thing I know I'm on the beaches of Fishers Island, a man's wrist pressed to my mouth as I drank his blood."

He turned his head to look at her. "I spent the first century cursing my maker for saving me when no others survived. The second century coming to grips with who and what I was. The last century I have lived my life as I should, appreciating what is around me and attempting to help others."

She didn't see regret, only a man who had accepted his fate. If only she could be like him.

Why it was important she didn't know, but Fallon asked anyway. "Were you married?"

"Yes. And to answer your next question, I had two children, Elisha and Philip." He looked back to the heavens and she knew their conversation about his life was over. There was still so much more she wanted to know, but wouldn't intrude.

"What about you?" he asked, rolling on his side to look at her.

"Mother and Dad dead. Ex-husband moved on to another woman. Only living relative is a grandmother. I waited tables to make ends meet." Emotion tightened her throat. "That's where I met Chavez. He was charming, nice. We went out a couple of times, and then—" Damn. She still felt so vulnerable when she tried to talk about that night. She had to change the subject. "Adrian, you never told me what you suspected about Billy's abduction. I don't think it had anything to do with Chavez or me."

"I think you're right. Besides I would have felt him enter my territory." She heard the confidence and concern in his tone.

Adrian had no idea what comfort that brought Fallon. "Well?"

"It was someone I know—a vampire. Someone the land doesn't recognize as an enemy. You felt the protection spell around the boy. Whoever did this hadn't wanted the child to be harmed. So there lies the quandary. Why Billy? And for what purpose?"

It didn't make sense. Adrian's people had searched the house, outer barns and sheds for any foul play, but had found none.

It was true there were a few stray vampires in the vicinity, but he couldn't fathom why they would do such a thing since he had already checked them out and felt confident they had nothing to do with Billy's kidnapping.

"Maybe it was a really bad joke," Fallon offered.

A joke? No. He would stake a bet on it. Everything was done for a purpose. He just had to figure out what it was. Until then he had asked that the humans under his protection be constantly observed. Now he had to cope with Fallon and her independent attitude.

"Fallon, until this situation with Chavez is resolved I don't want you outside without an escort. Me."

She jackknifed into a sitting position. "You're kidding, right?" Before he could respond she continued, "Do you have any idea how long I've been taking care of myself? I can't simply hide."

"Isn't that what you've been doing? Hiding by running away?"

Anger chased pain across her face.

Dammit. He hadn't meant it quite that way. Problem with the truth was that at times it hurt more than a lie.

She pushed to her feet, briskly brushing leaves and grass from her backside. If silence was a gauge of how angry she was with him, then she must be pretty pissed because she didn't respond or look his way. She just disappeared in a thin line of mist.

Fallon was getting stronger. Where she had once been a light fog in the air, her only presence was a glassy shimmer as she hightailed it away from him.

She hadn't been gone long when Adrian felt the land tremble, heard the cry of resistance as something or someone evil landed upon it.

"*Adrian.*" Panic-stricken, Fallon screamed, "*Chavez—I feel him.*"

Bones ground, feathers sprung from his pores as he held the vision of a bird in his mind. "Come back to me, darlin'." He tried to convey a calmness he didn't feel as the transformation was complete. With a push of his powerful legs and a flap of his wings he rose into the air.

"*Briar.*" He called to his friend using the mind link between them. "*Chavez has arrived. Alert the others and join me.*"

"*Will do, Boss.*"

Dammit! Yesterday, he had discovered that Chavez had been seen in a little cantina in Juarez, Mexico, just across the border of El Paso. Mexico or Texas had been too close for comfort.

And now the bastard was here.

Chapter Seventeen

A familiar nausea swept over Fallon's misty form alerting her that Chavez was closing in on her. The air thickened with the rancid smell of evil and the spicy aftershave the devil wore to lure his victims to his side. Even the swirl of wind below her that raised fallen leaves, lifting them high into a vortex, didn't chase the ominous warning away.

Fallon was out of time. Chavez had found her.

Heart pounding, she could sense her enemy's feelers creeping like snakes in a pit, crossing one over another, in an attempt to locate her exact position. Her mental dodges only lasted so long. Her mind was an endless maze, twisting and turning. Each path she took, he barreled down it in search of her.

Chavez made connection.

Vertigo hit her hard and fast.

Land beneath her whirled and spun, throwing her off-balance and she fought desperately to get back to Adrian.

It was all too much. She wasn't ready to confront her demon. She wasn't strong enough—not yet.

The horror of Chavez's nearness shattered her composure. With a sudden dip she began to fall from the sky, descending at an ungodly speed that stole her breath. There was only a second to pull herself together—a second to shape-shift back into human form and soften her landing before she crashed to the ground.

With a thud, she still hit hard. The impact so great her knees buckled. Trembling, she jerked to her feet, stumbled and another wave of nausea pitched her forward and she bent at the waist. Sour and acidic, vomit threatened to crawl up her throat.

Survival meant getting to Adrian.

She gulped in a much needed breath that smelled and tasted unclean, as if the air itself had been poisoned. Even before the queasiness subsided, she straightened, determined to reach Adrian before Chavez found her. When she tried to run—command her legs to move—they wouldn't respond.

A strangled cry pushed from her diaphragm. "*Adrian. I can't move.*" Whether fear gripped her in its iron claws or Chavez's power, she didn't know. Icy fingers of dread slowly slid over her skin.

Cold. A shiver shot to her bones, shaking her entire body. She couldn't remember when she felt so cold.

"*I'm here.*" Fallon heard Adrian's soothing voice just prior to him materializing before her. Relief rushed over her. In a heartbeat she was in his arms. Strong and comforting, his warmth melted some of the numbness that had overtaken her.

"*Ahhh… Cómo muy es dulce.*" Chavez's Spanish accent made Fallon jerk her head from Adrian's shoulder. She moved so quickly that pain splintered up her neck as she wrenched around to see her tormentor not more than twenty feet away. "How very sweet," he repeated in English.

Fallon had almost forgotten how breathtakingly attractive he was at first sight. Just under six feet, Chavez wore a rakish, debonair aura.

Couple that with his caramel skin tone and his seductive accent, and he could bewitch any woman.

It had worked on Fallon.

She closed her eyes, mentally shaking her head to chase the memories away, but they broke down her barriers and flooded into her mind anyway.

Soft music in the background, the elegant restaurant, Chavez charming and holding her hand across the table. What he offered was a better life for her and Christy. What she got was a living hell.

The reminder ripped her eyelids open.

Chavez brushed his long, genteel fingers through his black, shoulder-length wavy hair. Fingers she knew could go from seductive to cruel in less than a heartbeat. He stood masked as a gentleman in his trendy black slacks and white silk shirt, but she saw past his veneer and into a soul as black as coal.

Beauty truly was skin deep. Even if it came disguised as a handsome, captivating and intelligent man—deadlier than any mass murderer the world had ever seen.

Dark, gray clouds formed high above him, as if marking the spot where evil dwelled. A low, menacing rumble quaked, before slivers of light raced from one dark spot to the next.

Adrian's grip tightened around Fallon. She could feel tension driving her fingernails into his skin, but he didn't flinch or release her.

Instead his eyes narrowed. "Chavez, you arrived in my territory unannounced and unwelcome."

A hand to his heart with an expression of sadness, Chavez feigned being wounded by Adrian's words. "Not so, *mi amigo. Mi belleza* surely explained I would soon appear to bring her home."

To an outsider Chavez might have appeared as a man looking for his lost love. He stroked her body with a warm, sexual gaze. Then he extended his hand to her.

Fallon could feel the beginning ripples of his power slide up her spine. God, she hated the moment when the soft prickles turned to punishing knives that struck every tender nerve. Within her mind she would fight him, but physically she didn't stand a chance.

Memories of beatings, torture, the immoral ways he used her body, and Christy's death—made Fallon press closer into the shelter of Adrian's body.

"*Venido a mí, mi belleza.*" She hated the way he called her "my beauty" as he beckoned her to him.

With just a thought he invaded her mind and pushed so that her head splintered into shards of pain. Her hands jackknifed to her temples. The fluttering in her mind sounded as if thousands of bats were released in the small confines. Each of them whispering, "Come to me, my beauty," louder and louder, over and over.

Chavez's compulsion was strong, overbearing. It pulled at her—drawing her with the force of a magnet. As she mentally struggled to remain in Adrian's embrace, her arms and legs did just the opposite, kicking and striking out for release.

"Nooo…" she cried, desperately.

Chavez innocently widened his eyes. A look of concern fell across his handsome features. "What? You are not happy to see me? *Mi belleza…*" His tone was sweet, too sweet, as it lowered. "I have missed you terribly."

Adrian's hold never wavered. "Cut the pretense, Chavez. Fallon doesn't want to go with you."

Fallon was caught in a mass of chaos, a war between body and mind. Adrian's strength surrounded her, giving her the feeling of safety, while Chavez did just the opposite.

Chavez's taunting laughter cut across Fallon's skin, coarse and brittle. "If this is true, then why does she fight you to be at my side?"

Fallon felt Adrian's healing powers against the agony in her head and the pain tightening every muscle and tendon in her body. Slowly and consistently, he worked to counteract what Chavez's evilness wreaked.

Her skin was clammy. Perspiration beaded across her body. Several drops rolled between her breasts. If it wasn't for Adrian's taut grip she would have slid down his body to collapse on the forest floor.

"You are stronger than you realize. Do not wait for his attacks. Prepare yourself mentally for his invasions," Adrian coached, using the link between them. *"My blood runs through your veins. He cannot defeat you—not with me by your side."*

It started small inside her, a light burning brighter and brighter, as Adrian's strength grew. He filled her with such awesome power that she straightened, her shoulders pushing back as her head rose.

The façade Chavez wore slipped as he scrutinized Fallon's new confidence. His lips parted. Slowly, his chin dipped, his eyes darkening with awareness as the two of them embraced. "You have taken what is mine, and mine alone—twice." It wasn't a question but an accusation. One that left Fallon a little confused. If he was talking blood and sex, then he was a little short on the numbers.

Not to mention, how the hell did he know?

A woman's whimper drew both Fallon's and Adrian's attention to a cluster of trees where two vampires dressed in black held Doreen by her arms. Tears tracked down her cheeks. Blood oozed from a busted lip. The condition of her mussed hair and ruffled clothing, bruises and blood, revealed she'd been roughed up pretty badly.

"Adrian, I'm sorry." Her hoarse voice was almost non-existent. "Billy—"

She groaned, deeply and painfully, folding at the waist as if something hard and swift struck her abdomen.

Casually, Chavez strolled to where his vampire minions held Doreen. With his knuckles he skimmed her swollen cheek. Then he moved so quickly his actions were a blur. Grabbing a handful of her hair he snapped her head up.

Panic-stricken, Doreen stared wide-eyed. Frightened, animalistic sounds tore from her throat as she fought against the two vampires who began to snicker, "*bebé pobre.*" Poor baby, Fallon translated. She had never met these two abominations. Yet they were Spanish like their leader and appeared just as cruel as they taunted Doreen. One fondled the woman's breast, then squeezed her nipple so hard that she screamed out in pain. Their evil laughter made Fallon's skin prickle.

She felt Adrian release his power, but he was too late.

"Bitch," Chavez snarled as he sank his teeth into Doreen's tender throat. He jerked his head back, ripping skin and muscle, leaving a gaping wound that gushed her life essence.

Her eyes were wild with fear. She tried to scream, but it caused the blood to pump faster from the wound, producing soft, wet gurgling sounds.

Adrian's force struck hard, wrenching Chavez off his feet and sending him crashing into a tree, at the same time he spoke to Doreen. "*Shut down your heart. Save your strength and blood.*"

As Doreen attempted to obey Adrian, Fallon felt Chavez give the woman a command to stay conscious. "*You shall bleed slowly to your death,*" he promised, low and threatening on the mind path he shared with Doreen and Fallon.

An intentional move to let Fallon know her death would be next. She could feel his excitement mixed with fury. Electricity in the air sizzled with the evilness coursing through his veins.

Hatred smoldered in Chavez's fiery eyes, his good looks mangled with madness as he glared at Doreen. "Release *mi marioneta,*" he demanded of his minions, coming to his feet with ease. "My puppet." The slight lift of his lips was cruel and sinister as he faced Doreen. "You evaded me for more years than I care to recall." He turned back around to face Adrian. Resentment thickened the air.

Doreen's blood covered Chavez's mouth, his fangs. Droplets of the crimson liquid smeared his white silk shirt, spreading as more dripped from his parted lips.

Shit! Adrian resisted the urge to run to Doreen's side. The woman's eyes had been so pleading. An apology? Had she been responsible for Billy's abduction? Was Doreen working with Chavez? Even still he couldn't just leave her to die.

"*Dammit, Briar, where are you?*" Adrian needed assistance to get both Doreen and Fallon to safety before he took care of Chavez and his minions. He had no doubt Chavez would fall this night, but his first instincts were to safeguard the women.

"*Just clearing the treetops, Boss.*" A spot against the cloudy sky announced Briar's approach. Behind him Cougar, Tucker, and two more of the men from the ranch, Shorty and Dillon. Additional help would come if need be, but Adrian didn't want to involve any more of his people than necessary.

As his friends took human form, Adrian felt the Master vampire quietly probe him for weaknesses. He could feel the jabs of inquiry building in strength with Chavez's frustration at the new arrivals. His vampire minions stirred restlessly, until he nailed them with a glare.

Adrian had scanned Chavez's memories the minute he had experienced the quiver in the land. Chavez felt he was invincible. That would be his downfall.

Chavez's expression softened in an almost friendly appearance as he faced Adrian, but his eyes didn't, revealing the truth behind them. He was furious. Still his body language was contradictory. Elbows tucked to his side, he raised his hands, palms up, and shrugged. "*No vine buscando apuro.*"

"Not looking for trouble? Yeah. Sure." Skeptical, Tucker moved beside Adrian.

Chavez didn't spare a glance toward Tucker or any of the other men, instead he focused on Fallon. "*Mi belleza,* I have missed your kisses." There was a sexy purr to the man's voice.

Adrian felt the tremor that assailed her as Chavez sent another compulsion weaving through her mind. Adrian used his own power to weaken Chavez's control on Fallon, but he could feel Doreen reaching out to him.

"*Doreen is fading. We need to move quickly.*" He used his people's mental path as he split his voice to speak aloud to Chavez in unison. "You know the law. If you kill in my territory—you'll be next." His words were a dark, cold promise.

"*Perdóneme.*" Chavez's tight smile was cruel and dangerous. "You quote me the law?" Blood trickled down the corner of his mouth. "These women are mine."

Fallon squared her shoulders. "You sick son of a bitch."

He feigned innocence. "*¿Yo?*"

"Yes, you!" Fallon spat, her face reddened with anger. Adrian could hear red-hot fury swishing through her veins. "You killed my baby." Her rage was so strong she shook from head to toe.

An expression of confusion drew his brows down. "I gave you freedom to join me. Live as an immortal, but you fought me at every turn."

In disbelief, her mouth parted. Her eyes widened. "Freedom," she repeated. "You think taking from me the only person I loved in this world meant freedom to me?"

"*Sí.*"

She pushed from Adrian's embrace, her fists clenching and releasing. "You'll never hurt another being again." The rapid rhythm thundering in her chest matched her breathing, labored and tight. He knew she had to get it all out before she could start to heal.

"*Good girl.*" The woman Adrian had come to know surfaced with both barrels loaded. Her anger had chased away her fear. He could feel her confidence growing.

What he hadn't expected was her sudden attack, lunging with preternatural speed straight for Chavez's throat.

Chavez was quick, throwing up an invisible wall that Fallon struck hard with a resonating thud. The impact flung her back and into Adrian's arms, throwing him off balance and they both hit the ground. He heard her breath join his as it whooshed from their lungs. She didn't stir, hanging limp in his embrace. He had only a moment to assess that she was merely unconscious, when Chavez lowered his shield, preparing to attack.

With blazing speed Adrian jumped to his feet, ensuring his body was between Fallon and their enemy.

In seconds the vampire minions closed in around their leader, taking a protective stance. Briar and Tucker followed suit next to Adrian. Cougar's form simply disappeared into thin air.

Chavez hesitated a fraction of a second as if he questioned whether to fight with the odds against him.

"*Get Doreen,*" Adrian ordered Shorty and Dillon.

When Chavez saw their intentions, he snapped his gaze from Fallon to Doreen. The corner of his lip rose baring his teeth, as he snarled, "She's mine." Before he could reach Doreen, Cougar reappeared, blocking his approach.

With a lift of his chin, Chavez raised his face to the sky. Tendons bulged as if they would burst in his throat. He released a bloodcurdling scream that shook the treetops. Lightning zigzagged in a strange pattern across the heavens. He trembled with fury. Then he pinned Adrian with a hot glare. "You have not made a friend of me this night." His warning was issued with eerie calm. With a push of his powerful legs he shot into the sky, his minions following as the clouds opened and swallowed them up.

Tucker and Briar both lunged into the sky after Chavez.

"Stop!" At Adrian's command the two men hovered above him mid-air. "It's a trap. Electrical netting. Chavez wants us to follow."

The heat of battle raged through his friends' veins as it did his, but it was too late. The spider-web of lightning that continued to flash gave away the vampire's trap.

Adrian knelt down to pick Fallon up in his arms. "The fight is over for tonight."

But Doreen's fight for life was not.

Chapter Eighteen

The following evening Fallon woke with the headache from hell. The consistent throb felt like someone beat upon her brain with a sledgehammer. Lethargically, she gave a mental push sending rich soil spraying into the air as she rose into the air.

Unexpected pain greeted her. She couldn't lift her arms—didn't try—as a spasm tightened every inch of her body.

"Ow-ow-ow," she muttered, trying to comprehend why she hurt so badly.

In a silent plea she requested the elements to cleanse her nakedness. It always made her feel better, she thought, praying for relief as she drifted down to the ground. The coolness of the dirt met her bare feet, but even that made her clench her teeth.

"What happened?" she wondered, because it felt like she'd been caught in a stampede.

With a quick scan of the room she discovered Adrian was nowhere to be seen. She was alone with her memories and they were vague at best. The last thing she remembered was a red haze filling her head and the thought of Chavez's death.

As she moved, pain splintered across her right shoulder. "Ow," she cried again, cringing at the large black and blue area. Damn if it didn't feel as if she'd been kicked by a horse.

Why wasn't her natural healing kicking in?

Every step she took was a chore as she slowly and carefully headed toward the stairs. Even attiring herself in a short, flimsy dress of silk and matching sandals was a monumental task.

This was ridiculous. She hurt all over.

"Damn you, Adrian." This had his interference written all over it.

"Cursing me?" The sound of his deep, sexy voice jerked her head up allowing a prickly sensation to rush down her neck. An imposing figure, he stood at the top of the stairs staring down at her with an expression of anger on his handsome face. The downward dip of his full lips was a dead giveaway he wasn't happy with her. He confirmed her suspicion when he said, "What the fuck were you thinking?" The deep reprimanding growl set her on edge.

"Thinking?" she repeated skimming her gaze from his booted feet, up tight fitting jeans that gave her pause at a rather impressive bulge, and a T-shirt that molded his chest like it was making love to him. Cowboy hat pulled down low on his forehead

"Oh, yeah. That's right. You weren't," he lashed out like a whip. She felt the sting of his words. "Dammit, Fallon." He yanked his hat off and ran his long fingers through his hair. "You could have gotten us all killed."

Understanding took second place to the pain she felt. She groaned, raising one foot and then another climbing toward him. Her calves hurt. Her thighs hurt. Every place on her body ached. When she finally spoke, exasperation laced her words. "Adrian, I don't know what you're talking about."

His frown deepened. "You don't remember attacking Chavez?"

She felt her eyes pop open, as she pulled to a stop halfway up the stairs. "Me?" Her sandals flapped against the next step as she moved toward him.

He stepped back as she reached the final stair and let her pass. "Yeah. You." His warm breath caressed the side of her neck awakening her hunger. Damn he looked good, smelled good too, masculine heat warmed by his temper. And he was definitely in a snit this evening.

"All I remember is Doreen— Oh my God." She spun around to face him, sending another ache from one extremity to the other. "Is she okay?"

Adrian's expression hardened. "She didn't make it. I was too late to save her."

The news of the woman's death sent a chill through her veins.

Chavez had killed another innocent person.

Unshed tears ached behind her eyelids. Would the pain and suffering the demon inflicted ever stop?

Fallon reached out to Adrian wanting and needing to console him, but he shunned her grasp and headed down the hall. She attempted to touch his mind, but she met a wall of resistance.

At a loss for what to say, she murmured, "I'm sorry."

"You don't remember anything about last night?" He brushed her sympathy off by redirecting the subject. But she knew what his people meant to him. He was suffering, even if he did so in silence and alone.

Yes. She remembered Doreen's panic-stricken expression as death hung over her, the cruelty in Chavez's eyes, and the red-hot hatred she felt before everything went black.

Did Adrian blame her for Doreen's death?

Still presenting her with his back as he briskly moved through the house, he huffed, "Well, darlin', you didn't wait for me to handle the situation." He glanced over his shoulder. "You jumped headfirst into trouble and trouble's what you got." His breathy sigh held irony as he opened the kitchen door and stepped inside.

Fallon's emotions felt raw lying just below the surface. She hastened her steps to catch up with him. "Chavez got away? He isn't dead?" Her questions were met with silence and a room full of weary eyes.

Gary sat at the picnic table with Tucker, Briar, and Cougar. Maggie was consoling Crystal as she softly cried. Sally and Susan leaned quietly against the counter. The creak of the back screen door sounded as George entered, going straight to Susan and taking her into his arms.

They mourned the loss of their friend.

"I'm so sorry for your loss," Fallon whispered.

Sally approached her, gathering her hand in hers. "Doreen was a sweet girl. We'll miss her." She squeezed Fallon's hand before releasing it.

"*Adrian, was your friend's death my fault?*" Fallon couldn't stand the pause before he responded.

"*No. The damage Chavez did to her throat couldn't be repaired. She lost too much blood.*"

"So Doreen was responsible for Billy's abduction," George stated matter-of-factly.

"What?" Fallon couldn't hide her surprise as her voice rose.

With a hip against the refrigerator, his arms crossed over his chest, Adrian offered an explanation. "Evidently you and Doreen were both running from Chavez's tyranny."

Before he could say more Crystal raised her head from Maggie's shoulder. "I didn't know what she intended to do. I swear." Her eyes were red and swollen from tears that continued to flow down her cheeks. "When Doreen discovered Chavez was after Fallon, she panicked. She found something in Adrian's blood that allowed her to shield herself from Chavez for the last ten years. But she knew Fallon was young, lacked the experience to avoid Chavez." She gulped down a breath. "Doreen thought Billy's disappearance would be blamed on Fallon or at least chase her away." Remorse dulled the brunette's eyes as she glanced at Fallon. "I'm sorry."

"No, I'm the one who should be apologizing." Inadvertently, Fallon had caused Doreen's death. The fact sent chills down her spine. "If I hadn't stayed none of this would have happened."

"Hush," Sally admonished, "I don't want to hear any more of that. What's done is done."

"Sally's right." Adrian pushed away from the refrigerator and crossed the room. "No one leaves this house without my consent." He spoke to everyone, but his eyes were pinned on Fallon.

"Adrian—"

He held up a single hand silencing her. "Fallon, not one step outside this door."

Damn. She hated it, but he was right. It went against her grain to let someone else fight her battles. Still, she wasn't an idiot. Chavez was too powerful for her. She would be walking straight to her death or something worse if he caught her.

Five steps and Adrian stood before the back door. "Now I need to speak with Cougar, Briar, Tucker, Gary and George." As he opened it, the familiar creak sounded and a rush of clean night air filled the kitchen.

Tucker was the last one out, but before he closed the door he turned toward Maggie. "No one leaves this house."

The redhead released a frustrated breath. "Damn man."

For a moment there was silence among the women. It seemed that everyone was at loss for words, until Sally said, "I have work to do." She swiped her hands on a dish towel lying on the counter, reached for a canister and opened it to sprinkle a little flour on a cutting board. "How about I whip up some cinnamon rolls for tomorrow's breakfast?"

Susan turned to Fallon. "It quiets Mom's nerves to cook." She strolled to her mother's side. "Let me help you."

"It's been a while, but if you need more help I could probably manage rolling the dough," Fallon offered. What else was she going to do confined to the house?

"Sugar's in the pantry. Brown sugar, too," Susan added, as she opened a cabinet and retrieved a box of raisins, salt, and cinnamon.

Maggie and Crystal took seats at the picnic table, remaining quiet.

The distinctive smell of yeast added to warm water filled the kitchen as Sally began to prepare the dough. The gentle sounds of flour, sugar, and other ingredients being measured and placed in a bowl touched Fallon's ears. With her heightened sense of smell she focused on the cinnamon, hot and spicy. There was something seductive about the scent which made her think of Adrian.

Although he had stated Doreen's death wasn't her fault, why had he treated her so indifferently this evening?

And what about Chavez? Where was he? And more importantly, when would he strike again?

Apprehension skittered across her skin, but not paralyzing fear that crippled her so she couldn't move.

"No bad dreams this morning," Susan stated cautiously glancing askance toward Fallon. Everyone else's eyes followed. "Are you feeling better?"

The woman was right.

"Yes," Fallon whispered, realizing for the first time in a year and a half she hadn't dreamed of Christy nor had she awakened screaming or crying.

Why?

And why wasn't she frozen with fear or overcome with rage when she thought of Chavez? Once again she wondered why she still felt the aches of last night's events. Was it Adrian's doings or Chavez's?

"Adrian will handle this man who seeks you," Sally said with confidence. "You won't have any more trouble after tonight."

True. If Adrian succeeded Fallon would be free. If he didn't then she was dead—really dead. Either way she would be with Christy come the morning.

Relief and sadness blended to a confusing level. Fallon was ready to confront Chavez, ready to put an end to the running and the anguish she felt. Even still something tugged at her heart when she thought of leaving Adrian.

Damn if she hadn't fallen in love with the man.

The land shook and wept when Chavez and his minions emerged from it. Evil had a way of upsetting the natural balance of the elements. Adrian had felt the disturbance beneath his feet earlier, but he had been too far away to intercept them.

Chavez was good. He covered his tracks well. But the vampire wouldn't evade Adrian forever.

For a moment, he stood quietly and listened to the soft chanting of the Apaches. The gentle breeze carried their voices, as well as the smell of burning pine from their campfires. Songs of healings and blessings echoed as they prayed to ancient spirits. The people of the White Mountains believed that beyond the physical world was the spirit world or the world of unseen powers. Harmony with nature and acceptance of that world were central to life. When harmony was out of balance, then life too was disproportionate.

Peace was what they sought.

But to achieve such, Adrian would have to rid the world of Chavez.

"Three deaths have been reported." Briar moved beside Adrian as he stared out into the forest. "Campers along White River. The brutality was so vicious it's been attributed to a bear."

Anger rose swiftly in Adrian. It burned through his veins, heating his blood. Doreen. Now three more innocent people were dead. Chavez's killing spree would not end. It was the vampire's way of taunting Adrian—murdering in his territory.

And with each kill Chavez's power strengthened. Adrian could sense it growing.

"I can't allow this to go past tonight. We finish it before the sun rises." His thoughts wandered toward Fallon, but he jerked them back in line. He had to stay focused, had to stay alert. He would not fail.

Adrian sent mental tentacles across the land in search of Chavez. "Any news from Cougar?" Unrest cried upon the wind whistling through the trees. Their branches shook as if attempting to rid the evil that touched them.

"Not yet," Tucker replied, pulling his hat down low. "But all the vampires from around the valley have checked in. They're alert and in place throughout the various towns, ready to mask any further carnage or to come to your aide if you need them."

Adrian could sense Tucker's concern for Maggie. Adrian felt the same for Fallon, as well as all the people beneath his protection.

Suddenly his tentacles of power struck something so evil that it shook Adrian to the core. Dark and menacing, he smelled the poisonous vapors thickening the air, felt the cold, sinister touch of Chavez.

"It's time." Adrian released a weighted breath. "Let's hunt."

Chapter Nineteen

"*Mommy.*"

The soft, familiar cry brought Fallon to her feet. Pain erupted across her bruised shoulder and other parts of her abused body. Her pulse sped with the thudding of her heart against her chest.

Christy.

"*Mommy, I need you*," her daughter's small voice cried. The sound was distant as if it came from beyond the brick and mortar of the house.

"*Mommy.*"

Goose bumps raced across Fallon's arms as she rushed to the living room window and stared into the darkness. Palms against the cool glass, her warm breath fogged the window. The muscles in her stomach clenched.

It was a trick—nothing more.

She tried to convince herself, but the need to run out the front door and find Christy was strong—overpowering.

"Is everything okay?" Maggie unfolded her legs from beneath her where she sat on the sofa reading a book. Crystal had gone to her room. Sally and Susan were icing the cinnamon rolls in the kitchen. Adrian and the others had never returned.

"Huh?" Fallon faced Maggie. "Yeah. Everything's okay." But it wasn't. Every nerve in Fallon's body was alive and tingling.

"*Mommy!*" Christy's cry was sharp and brittle. "*The bad man says he'll hurt me again, if you don't come to me now.*"

Fallon's mouth parted on a gasp. Her eyes grew moist. The fear in her child's trembling voice sounded so real, so compelling.

Maggie set her book down on the coffee table and pushed to her feet. "No. Everything is not okay." The woman's face grew taut. Her hands trembled. "He's here isn't he?" Her voice dropped to where it was almost a whisper of anxiety. "We need to call Adrian."

Fallon's internal struggle was pulling her in two directions. Her need to believe Christy was alive was so great, for a moment she started to disagree when—

"*Mi belleza, your daughter awaits you.*" Chavez's sexy Spanish accent called to Fallon.

She cringed. What an idiot she was.

"*Mommy, please…*" Fallon heard the desperation in Christy's plea.

She cupped her ears with her palms. "No, it isn't real. Stop."

Maggie's hand landed on her arm. "What? What isn't real? Fallon, you're scaring me."

"*Mi belleza, it is real. She has always been waiting for you. Always within my care.*"

"Liar. She's dead." Anger flared hot and fast across Fallon's cheeks. "You killed her, you fucking animal."

While Chavez used the mental link between them, Fallon spoke aloud, unaware of the result until a cry squeezed from Maggie's lips.

"I'm calling Adrian." Maggie's panicked tone joined Christy's and Chavez's voices in Fallon's head. *"Something's wrong with Fallon. Chavez is near."*

Adrian's unyielding voice followed. *"Stay put. Do not go outside."*

Feeling reassured that Adrian was near gave Fallon determination. This was only a trick to coerce her beyond Adrian's safety.

Chavez's laughter taunted her. *"Lie. Far from a lie. Right now my fingers are stroking the strands of her silky hair."* Fallon heard him inhale deeply. *"She smells so sweet…powdery like that of a baby."*

The memory of the baby shampoo Christy insisted on using made Fallon's knees buckle. "No." Pain crashed against her kneecaps as she landed on the hard wood flooring.

Maggie crouched, looping her arms around Fallon's shoulders. "He can't reach you here. Adrian's safeguards are too strong. I'll stay with you."

"Stop!" Christy screamed.

Fallon jerked to her feet and out of Maggie's embrace. Christy's cries were small, broken whimpers tearing at Fallon's heart.

Trick. Christy was dead. Fallon had to remember. She had seen her daughter's bloody, crumpled body on the floor of their apartment. No movement from her child, as Chavez had carried Fallon away kicking and screaming from their home. She had never seen Christy again.

"Ahhh… Mi pequeño bebé. Don't cry your madre will join us soon." The calmness in Chavez vanished, instead his impatience showed. *"Your daughter is immortal as we are. You can join us now or I will make sure her last breaths are not easy ones."*

It couldn't be true, Fallon told herself. Christy hadn't been alive all this time living beneath the cruelty of Chavez's hands.

Something flashed outside the window drawing Fallon's attention. Terror ripped through her sending ice shards through her veins. "Christy." Her daughter's name was only a breath. The child stood between Chavez and one of his minions in the lacy pink dress Fallon had purchased for her last birthday.

Without a second thought Fallon ran for the door, tore it open, and raced through it. In the back of her mind she heard Maggie call her name, Adrian's furious roar, but it was nothing compared to her daughter's tears. They echoed over and over in Fallon's head.

She flew into Christy's open arms, weeping.

As soon as she touched Christy, Fallon felt a thick cloud of evil surround her. Slowly she leaned back to gaze at her daughter's soft face. The beautiful smile that greeted her began to fade, as well as her delicate features that began to twist and contort along with her small body beneath Fallon's hands. She tried to push away, but Christy's grip was unyielding. Panic rose fast and ruthless, crashing into Fallon when she found herself in the arms of Chavez's second minion. The oily smell of his greased-back dark hair made her cringe. His breath was hot and foul, the stench of death, as his laughter brushed across her face. With a quick twist she was turned in the vampire's embrace, so she faced Chavez.

She cringed when he reached for her. His chuckle was sadistic, as he stroked her cheek making her stomach twist with pain. Lightly he ran a finger along her jawbone, tracing her features. "*Mi belleza*, how I have missed you. You are still the most beautiful woman I have ever seen." He offered her his crooked arm in invitation. "Shall we go home?"

Fallon released a heavy breath of resignation and linked her arm with his. There was nothing left of her life. She would seek death no matter the struggle. It was a waiting game, she would win. Either way she took comfort in knowing that Chavez was a dead man. For the deaths he had taken on Adrian's soil, Chavez would die. Adrian would never give up until it was so.

And then, Fallon's revenge would be complete.

The roar that tore from Adrian's diaphragm when he saw Fallon dissolve before his eyes had everyone around him taking a step backward. Dread like he had never known before swelled up inside and threatened to consume him. He couldn't lose Fallon—not now when he had found his only true love. A woman who completed him so thoroughly she felt like the very air he breathed.

Maggie pushed open the front door of the house and ran to meet them. "Adrian, he tempted her with a child—a little girl." She shook, even as Tucker gripped her hands to still the tremors. "It-it was heartbreaking to see her flee into the child's arms." Horror stole Maggie's voice as her tone turned frantic. "But it was all an illusion. Oh my God. That beautiful child didn't exist. Instead it was one of Chavez's minions in disguise."

"Christy," Adrian whispered more to himself than any one else.

Maggie's green eyes gaped. "Yes. That's the name Fallon screamed as she ran from the house."

"Christy was Fallon's daughter. Chavez killed the child and then enslaved Fallon." The group of people surrounding Adrian grew quiet—deathly quiet.

Briar broke from the group. "What do you want us to do, Boss? How do we get your woman back?"

"We can't rush him. We saw what happened to Doreen." The memory made Adrian weak in the knees. Just the thought of not waking each morning with Fallon was driving him wild. When he imagined what Chavez would do to her—

He shook his head driving the pictures from his mind. There was no way he would lose Fallon to Chavez.

No way.

Slowly he released his magic, allowing it to stroke the land, requesting its assistance to locate Fallon. Within seconds his senses jumped as if lightning struck one nerve and then another. He could feel Fallon's acquiescence—feel her despair. But strangely he also felt peacefulness surrounding her, an emotion he didn't understand. He started to reach out to her, but instead pulled back. Better no contact than to allow Chavez to know how close they would be very soon.

"They're in the sacred caves." A maze of man-made caves and caches were carved by the Apaches many years ago used for shelter from the cold and their enemies. It was a sacred place hidden from view that he and Cougar had visited to bless the earth on many occasions. One could stare right at the entrances and never see them.

How Chavez had stumbled upon them Adrian had no idea.

Familiar pain washed over him as he began to shape-shift into a large black bird. Cougar, Tucker, and Briar followed suit and together they rose into the air.

Beneath them the sing-song Indian tongue of his human friends began a chant. "Ai-Ai-Ai." Softly at first their voices sang, and then louder as they called upon the spirits of the creator to come to their aid.

Adrian knew they would need all the help they could get.

Fallon hadn't even known the labyrinth of caves existed. They were cool and damp, as Chavez led the way through a network of winding pathways. A fresh breeze joined the smell of rich soil. There had to be many exits for such a strong current to exist. Something brittle popped beneath their feet. Once she almost fell, but the man behind her caught her then pushed her forward. Pain from the previous night's adventures and this evening's blurred to one large ache across her body. Chavez stopped at a place where water seeped through several crevices before creating a stream that flowed ahead of them into the darkness.

"You will wait here for us, *mi belleza.*"

As if she had a choice. His power ripped her arms from her sides, pinning them to the hard, uneven wall behind her. Next she felt her ankles secured. Just the thought of being alone, Chavez gone, gave Fallon peace of mind.

Then he pressed his mouth firmly to hers. She fought the urge to vomit knowing she would be harshly beaten or something worse. Instead she let him take what he wanted.

His triumphant grin was almost too much for her to bear.

"*Su entrega prueba tan dulce.*" The smacking sound he made as he placed his pinched thumb and forefinger next to his mouth made her tense. She knew enough Spanish to understand that he was rejoicing in her surrender, the taste of it so very sweet. "We must feed again before we leave this godforsaken country. You will miss me, *sí?*"

Yeah. Like a fucking hole in my head, she wanted to say. Instead she lowered her gaze and remained silent.

As he turned and walked away, Fallon couldn't help the tears that fell. She would never see Adrian again. Never feel his hands caressing her body, his kiss washing away the bitterness of Chavez's.

"*Adrian,*" she whispered not even attempting to hide the sorrow in her cry. There was no answer, and yet she knew he heard. Instead of a reply she felt a brush of power so strong she couldn't resist adding her own to it. Mental clicks went off in her head as her arms fell to her sides. In a second her ankles were freed.

"*Run, darlin'. Use the link between us to come to me.*" His warmth surrounded her with hope. If she could find her way out of the caves and to his side, maybe—just maybe she could feel his lips against hers one more time. The need to taste him gave her the energy she needed to try escaping Chavez once more.

Her keen sight helped her to see the twists and turns as she moved through the maze of caverns, but it was the thickened air and stench of evil that lead her out of the cave without any problems. A full moon brightened her path as she stepped into the night. She took a deep breath. Stars twinkled above her like nothing was amiss.

Sharp tingles raised the hair at the nape of her neck just as Chavez materialized before her.

A terrified scream tore from her throat.

With just a thought she dissolved into a fine mist and scattered. Quickly she planted some of her essence in a grove of trees like Adrian had taught her.

Evidence of another death dripped from Chavez's lips and teeth. His silky white shirt was splattered red. Fingers blood-stained, he raised them to his mouth and licked one and then the other slowly as if he savored the taste. He flashed an evil grin in the direction of the trees, as she continued to choose places to mislead him.

His eyes turned into darken holes, as she felt his anger rise. "Leaving so soon, *mi belleza?*" Handsome features melted into madness.

He stared cold and motionless, using his magic to rattle the treetops above her.

A flock of birds hiding within their branches scattered, their wings brushing against the air. Quickly Fallon climbed aboard one of them, pulling her essence from the trees and connecting them to the other fleeing birds.

Lightning erupted from a cloudless sky. One bird squawked before it exploded into flames and began to fall. Another splintered into a fiery mass as Chavez picked them off one after another out of the sky, until the only bird left in flight was the one she rode upon.

She pulled from the bird just as a flash of light incinerated it. The blast was so bright, so powerful that it knocked the vision of mist from her mind and she began to shape-shift midair. Sweat beaded her forehead as she dropped. Arms and legs flailed as she fought to take human form again. The thunder she heard was not in the sky, but her chest—heart pounding as the ground appeared to be rising fast to greet her.

She closed her eyes not wanting to see the death that awaited her.

A surprised squeak squeezed from her lungs as she was jolted to a stop. Warm, strong arms caught her and then gently placed her feet on the ground. When her eyelids rose she couldn't believe that Adrian held her. She threw her arms around his neck.

"Later," he whispered the promise, but she could hear the tension in his voice as he guided her behind him.

Chavez's eyes reddened with fury. His vicious fangs gnashed and clicked together. Spit and blood trickled from the corners of his mouth. With a roar he grabbed both sides of his shirt and tore, baring his chest heaving with his anger.

Fallon was shaking so hard her teeth chattered. She had seen Chavez mad, but never like this.

From the chaotic emotions of Chavez's rage and her fear came a confident, almost arrogant feeling from Adrian. Yet when he stepped forward to meet Chavez his face was void of all expression.

"You know the law," Adrian stated matter-of-factly. "You have wreaked havoc on my people. For that you will pay with your life."

The power and strength emanating from Adrian released like steam from a geyser. She felt it slam into Chavez and sling him across the ground as he attempted to touch her mind with a compulsion.

As Chavez scrambled to his feet, for the first time Fallon saw fear flash across his face, but was quickly replaced with a dauntless grin when his minions joined him.

"It is you that has broken the law. The woman is mine," Chavez reminded Adrian.

"Was," Adrian corrected firmly. "She's mine now."

Chapter Twenty

Adrian meant every word. Fallon was his. He would die to protect her.

A gust of wind rose quickly, lifting pine needles from the ground that were sharp missiles hurling toward him and Fallon.

"Stay behind me," he ordered, as a dozen or so penetrated his skin. The needlelike leaves stung as they burrowed deep. With a swipe of his hand he erected a barrier to repel the remainder. The sharp darts made snappy noises as they hit, bouncing off the invisible wall and falling to the ground.

"Give me back *mi belleza* and I will let you live." Chavez released a slow, ominous growl. "Resist me and you will die painfully, watching me devour her."

Just the thought tightened Adrian's resolve.

Already Chavez's minions had slid away from his side, moving into position to attack.

But Adrian knew one thing they didn't. Briar and Tucker had arrived. Their footsteps were silent, deadly, as they came to stand directly behind Chavez's men.

Ever the jokester, Tucker tapped the one before him on the shoulder. "Ready to party?"

Lightning fast, the vampire swung around and attacked.

The battle had begun.

Claws and fangs gnashed as the vampire fought to slit Tucker's throat. But Tucker was quick. As he darted away his cowboy hat flew off his head. He ducked and dodged like a boxer, left jab—right jab, leaving gaping cuts in the vampire's flesh with each strike. Tucker's feet were a blur as he shuffled about moving and separating his opponent away from the rest of the group. A light film of dust rose around their ankles, rising to encompass their knees.

Damn Tucker. He was playing with the man. Adrian felt Tucker's excitement, the thrill of the fight burning inside him. All his pent-up anger and worry he had felt for Maggie was being released. And Adrian sensed his friend wanted to make the most of this confrontation.

"Kill him and get it over with," Briar barked, his voice firm with impatience.

The vampire in front of Briar was dead before he knew what happened. Briar rammed his hand into the guy's chest. Adrian knew he held the vampire's heart in his hand when the Spaniard's eyes widened, pain splintering across his face. His entire body shook, as Briar raised him off his feet. Several brisk movements of his dangling feet and the fight vanished from the vampire. A sucking sound followed the withdrawal of Briar's hand from the vampire. He fell to the ground and erupted into flames on impact.

Chavez stood unmoving as he watched his minions die. His calm mask slipped—his face was red with fury.

"From the darkness of hell, I call to you." Chavez's voice shook with his rage. The earth trembled and mounds of black soil in five different locations rose around his feet. Like oil bubbling to the surface, they grew, stretching slowly until they measured at least seven feet long and about three feet wide. Then the ground shifted, taking form to create five separate human shapes with arms, legs and a head, except they appeared vaporous. He could see right through them to the grass and dirt beneath them.

"What are they?" Fallon's voice quivered. Cautiously, she stepped from behind Adrian. He carefully guided her back where she would be safe.

Adrian had never seen such beings before. "I don't know."

The opaque creatures slithered across the ground. Every place they touched grass and small plants withered and died leaving a blackened path behind them. A pair of them headed toward Briar and another in Tucker's direction.

Eerily, their gloomy figures rose to stand vertically, looming over each of the men. The last darkling remained beside Chavez as if he guarded him.

"Any ideas?" Tucker asked, a hint of nervousness edging his voice.

Adrian didn't have time to answer as the shimmering shadows fell across Tucker. He heard his friend gasp. Tucker's face went sheet white, as if the night creatures were sucking the very life out of him.

A strangled groan from Briar announced the creatures had attacked. As he swung around his razor sharp talons cut through his enemies without making a mark. It was like his hand passed through running water. The closer the darklings got to him the slower he appeared to be moving, until he stood paralyzed, struggling to raise his hands, to release his power. Ominously, the shadows swirled around him. Briar choked, his eyes widening. The demons were sucking the life from him.

Chavez thrust his hand out before him, curling his fingers.

"Adrian!" Fallon's cry made him glance over his shoulder as she grasped her neck. Whitened pressure points appeared where Chavez's invisible claw-like fingers wrapped around her throat.

Shit! Adrian had to think fast.

With all his strength, he raised Briar and Tucker from the ground, sending their bodies crashing into Chavez. All three men flew in different directions as they rebounded off each other.

The five dusky entities circled Chavez, guarding him as he rose. His anger resounded like thunder across the land.

Adrian could hear Fallon sucking in much needed breaths, as were Briar and Tucker as they slowly pushed from the ground to stand.

"We end this now." Adrian raised his hands to the sky, pulling down a gust of wind that whipped around Chavez's ankles stirring his pant legs.

Chavez's laugh was a husky whisper. "I expected more from you. Now return that which is mine." He jerked his outstretched hand to his chest and Fallon began choking, again. An invisible force raised her into the air and thrust forward, so that just the tips of her toes dragged through the pine needles, grass and dirt straight for Chavez and his guardians.

Briar's and Tucker's strength, though weakened, join his.

The flurry of air currents surrounding Chavez snapped and hissed, moving violently in a circular motion as they moved up his body, encompassing the darklings as well.

Adrian felt the hot and cold pockets that fed the gale. Winds spiraling inward sucked loose pine needles, leaves, debris into the air and even uprooted small trees as it drew upon its fury. He had to duck as a seedling whizzed by his head. In the distance, Briar and Tucker fell to the ground to avoid being hauled into the wrath of wind. Then

Adrian localized his anger and energy, focusing it around Chavez and his creatures.

Chavez roared, suddenly releasing his hold on Fallon. With a thud she fell to the ground. The groan forced from her throat was deep and long.

Pain once again radiated across Fallon's body. She crawled on hands and knees in time to witness panic flare across Chavez's face. The funnel cloud was smaller at the base, losing strength as it broadened at top where his shoulders and head were still visible. He tried to step from the cyclone revolving like a child's top around and around him, but he was tossed back and forth between the swiftly moving walls. The soft buzzing sound that had begun when the wind started was now loud and reverberating.

Desperately, Chavez moved one way and then the next to avoid his shadow people. As the tunnel of wind grew smaller and narrower, Chavez's creatures grew closer and closer to him, until they pressed against him and melted into his body.

Chavez screamed. The gurgling sound was terrifying. He was a drowning man gasping for that life sustaining breath, only to suck more water down his throat.

As the air shaft spun faster, it swallowed the air from the small confines of the twister.

Fallon saw his eyes bulge as he gripped his throat. His mouth parted.

Adrian's eyes were cold, dangerous as he approached Chavez.

He grew closer to the whirling mass. A strong breeze blew his hair about, but he appeared undaunted by the storm in front of him.

Power like Fallon had never seen before crackled like lightning around him, so thick she felt like she could reach out and touch it. Battle worn, Briar and Tucker stood erect lending their strength. The combination of their might together stole her breath.

The funnel completely engulfed Chavez, pulling him deeper into its fury.

The roar of the wind was so loud now it suffocated Chavez's screams.

All Fallon could see was this whirling haze.

Slowly. Deadly. Adrian raised his hand before him, as his fingertips extended into long, sharp talons.

"This is for Christy, Fallon, Doreen and all the others who have fallen beneath your cruelty." Cold intent hardened Adrian's features as he thrust his hand through the twister.

Time seemed to stand still as a ribbon of blood splattered in all directions, hitting everything in sight, including her. It was warm against her face and arms. But she couldn't keep her eyes off Adrian.

His power grew stronger not weaker.

The grayish volume of air continued to spin and whistle as if it were reaching a crescendo. Then Adrian extracted his hand from the funnel and everything seemed to die.

The energy in the air fizzled, so it was only a spark here and there.

The roar of the air current became a hum.

When the wind died down and the cyclone was gone, Chavez swayed. His bloody mass was unrecognizable as he crumbled to the ground.

Fallon watched Adrian as his fingers closed tightly into a fist, muscles and tendons taut in his arm. The loud explosion as Chavez shattered into flames before her eyes startled her. She jerked her gaze away. When she looked again there was nothing left of Chavez. But he had left his mark. The land was scorched and torn apart. It wept quietly in the breeze that carried the woodsy scent of the forest and the fresh smell of freedom.

Fallon released a weighted sigh.

Now Christy could rest peacefully.

Fallon was on her knees. Her red T-shirt was torn, hanging from one shoulder. Her jeans were spotted with black dirt. Eyes bloodshot and agape, she stared blindly at the spot where Chavez once stood. With each rapid rise and fall of her chest Adrian heard her ragged breaths. Her enemy's blood was splattered across her face and body, but she didn't seem to notice. Nor did she seem to realize he, as well as Tucker and Briar, were close by.

Very gently her shoulders began to shake. For a moment he thought she was crying until he heard a soft sound, giggles that turned into morbid laughter. At the same time tears began to stream down her face, and then she threw back her head and screamed. The cry tore from her diaphragm, raw and furious.

When she quieted, she glanced up at Adrian with so much pain on her face a lump formed in his throat. "I'm supposed to be happy, aren't I?" She hiccupped fighting the lack of oxygen.

"Ahhh… Darlin'." He moved before her and drew her up into his arms. He held her close.

"He's gone," she mumbled against his shoulder. "I thought I'd feel something—anything. But it doesn't bring Christy back." Her sobs deepened as she buried her face against his chest. Her fingers twisted his shirt as she clutched tightly to him. "Make the pain go away, Adrian. Make me not miss her so much. *Please…*"

His chest squeezed so firmly, he thought for a moment it would explode. "I wish I could, darlin'." He felt so fuckin' helpless. With all his strength and power he couldn't ease her sorrow. So he held her while she cried.

The wave of comforting thoughts Briar and Tucker wrapped around them didn't appear to help or ease the anguish seeping from her pores.

Silently his friends moved around the land cleaning up whatever evidence might be visible to the human eye. The stench of evil would remain until Mother Nature healed the land's wounds. But it wasn't as strong now that Chavez was gone and a cool breeze blew through the tree branches. When Briar and Tucker were finished they approached hesitantly.

"Adrian? You want us to wait?" Briar cleared his throat and look toward the sky.

"Fallon. Honey." Adrian raised her chin with a finger so their gazes met. "We need to go home. It will be light soon."

"Light?" she repeated. A shudder trembled through her. She furrowed her forehead, little worry lines appearing. Her grip on him loosened.

A ghost of apprehension slid across his skin. "Don't even think about it."

"Adrian—"

He pressed a finger to her lips. "No. I didn't fight the devil himself to lose you now."

She stepped back out of his embrace. "You don't understand."

He took her by the arms and couldn't help the little shake he gave her. Whether it was anger or fear he didn't know.

"I understand more than you know." Emotion surfaced so quickly it startled him. It traveled across his shoulders tightening muscles and tendons as it raced up his neck. "Remember, I outlived my family and friends." *Dammit. I won't let you go.* "I watched my wife and children mourn my death. I lost everything I loved that day. Don't you think it tore my heart out to see her marry my best friend? But I wanted her safe and happy, my children to have a father." He hadn't realized how very lonely he'd been these years until this moment.

Everything had changed when Fallon came into his life. "Don't you think Christy wants the same for you?"

Silent tears spiked her dark eyelashes. "I don't know what to think. I'm so confused. I miss Christy so much."

"Well know this, Fallon McGregor—I love you." He pulled her into his arms. "And I'll move heaven and earth to keep you in my arms." Then he captured her mouth in a fiery kiss.

Chapter Twenty-One

Adrian's mouth was fierce, hot and ruthless, demanding Fallon's complete surrender. Part of her wanted to yield, to give in to what he offered. But her promise to Christy haunted the back of her mind. Even now as he pressed his body so close to hers, new tears beat behind her eyelids for what she had lost and would be losing when she left him.

He broke the kiss, but still held her in a grip that said he'd never let her go.

Tender emotion glistened like amber lights in his eyes. "Stay with me." Voice husky, he added, "I need you." Although his friends stood a short distance away, Adrian didn't attempt to soften his tone or hide his feelings. Not only his love and need for her, but that of his family. Memories that felt so precious to Fallon.

It humbled her.

He was an extraordinary man. If he could live centuries and overcome his guilt and regret, could she? There had to be more to life then what fate had dealt her.

Fallon softened before she could help herself. "Yes. I'll stay." She prayed Christy would understand.

Adrian's eyes tightened a little at the corners as a full smile touched his lips. He looked happy. For the first time she noticed the blood that streaked his handsome features.

Chavez's blood.

It covered them both from head to toe. Her shirt was torn, hanging from one shoulder. Her jeans were in a little better shape. With just a thought, she cleansed traces of her enemy from her and Adrian's bodies, refreshing their clothing. Someday maybe she could erase Chavez from her mind just as easily.

"Adrian, take me away from this place."

"Anything you want, darlin'." He turned and addressing Briar and Tucker, he said, "Boys, let's go home."

Fallon could feel the strain of morning approaching as she shape-shifted into her Gyrfalcon form. As she lunged into the thinning darkness, she heard Briar say, "An Artic bird?"

"That's my girl." Adrian's deep laughter warmed her heart.

Soon Adrian and his friends were airborne, soaring alongside her. They were magnificent in flight. Majestic. She couldn't help remembering how they fought Chavez, his minions, and the creatures from the earth. It had been an awe inspiring sight to behold when they unleashed their power.

For so long Fallon hadn't felt safe, but surrounded by Adrian and his friends she did.

As they flew over the beautiful landscape of the White Mountains, past its valleys, lakes and creeks, she knew her decision to stay with Adrian and not seek the light was right. She loved Christy. But she also loved Adrian.

From high above the treetops, she could see the tile roof of Adrian's house. As giant birds, they each swept low and shape-shifted as their feet touched the ground. At once the yard was filled with people welcoming them home.

A concerned look on her face, Maggie ran to Fallon's side. "Are you okay?" She reached out and hugged Fallon. "Is it over?"

Fallon returned her new friend's embrace with a tight squeeze. "It's over." Thank God, it was truly over.

The jovialness Fallon had seen in Tucker earlier vanished as his boots pounded the ground toward them. "Why the hell aren't you aground?" he barked, addressing Maggie.

"Why the hell aren't you?" Maggie tossed back to him with an exasperated expression.

"Hurry inside," Sally warned as the bright orange-yellow rays of the sun peeked over the mountaintops. As everyone filtered into the house, Maggie and Tucker continued to bicker. They were still arguing as Adrian and Fallon descended the stairway to their resting place.

Each footfall felt leaden as she stepped from the stairs to the soil beneath her feet. With a brush of Adrian's hand he prepared the ground. A spray of dirt rose into the air, coming to rest in a pile beside the hole. The smell of freshly turned soil teased and tempted Fallon's nose.

With just a thought he ridded them both of their clothing. "Tired?" he asked. The damp coolness of the underground cave caressed Fallon's nakedness. With ease he lowered himself into their bed.

Mentally and physically she was worn out. "Yes." The aches and pains of the last few days still had a lingering effect on her.

He lay down against the welcoming soil, his arms outstretched. "Come here."

She went willingly into his embrace.

Gently, he pressed his lips to her forehead. "Sleep, darlin'." She felt his compulsion just before the beat of her heart stilled.

CR&O

Adrian woke Fallon with a kiss. He tasted her first breath on his lips, as he planned to do every rising. Hungry and aroused, it took all his control not to ravish her the minute she stirred.

He loved this woman.

Dark lashes rose as she opened her eyes and greeted him. "Hi, cowboy." She sounded sleepy and sexy, her sweet voice filling him with joy.

"Evening, darlin'." He smoothed his hand down her thigh, moving across her hip to settle upon her abdomen. "How do you feel tonight?" Damn good to him. She was soft beneath his palm.

Fallon gave him a confused look. "Feel?"

He brushed her hair off her shoulders and pressed his lips to the area where a nasty bruise had been. She had healed nicely, but that wasn't what he was talking about.

"No dreams?" he asked, as his hand cupped her perfect breast.

Her eyes widened. Whether it was realization dawning or the fact he began to roll her nipple between his fingers he didn't know.

"No dreams," she murmured. A soft smile curved her lips. She arched into his hand. "This is the second night in over a year and a half." She groaned, "Thank you."

He didn't have to ask for what. It shone in the sparkle of hope glistening in her eyes.

There had been a brief moment of worry when he awakened wondering if she would regret her decision to stay with him. But the calmness in her demeanor, the tender expression on her face said it all.

She was his forever.

His lips traveled a path over her shoulder blade, up her neck, until he reached her mouth. "If you're as good as new, what do you say about giving this cowboy a ride?"

Her laugh was hearty, more carefree than he had ever heard. "An eight second ride?"

"Hell, no." He rose, extending his hand to her as he stepped from their resting place. When her fingers closed around his he couldn't believe that she was truly his. "This cowboy likes to be ridden hard and put up wet—real wet." With just a thought he called to the elements to cleanse them both of the soil that dusted their naked bodies.

In a flash, she took off toward the stairs, giggling. "Then what are you waiting for?"

His feet thudded against the wood as he chased her like some randy high school boy. What a sight they must be, bare assed, running upstairs to his bedroom where his king-size bed awaited them. He couldn't remember when he had felt so lighthearted, couldn't remember when he wanted a woman as much as he did Fallon.

When he caught her just inside the bedroom, he jerked her into his arms. Her laughter was music to his ears. As their eyes met, the heat of the moment thickened, and her laughter died.

Her expression grew tight, serious. "Kiss me." She paused for a moment as if she wanted to say more, but kept the words to herself.

With a tilt of his head, he possessed her with a firm kiss. A nudge of his tongue against the seam of her lips, she opened to him and he plunged in. She tasted of a future, one filled with adventure, happiness, and love.

Never breaking their kiss, he eased her toward the large bed against the wall. When the back of her legs bumped the edge, he pushed her down upon the comforter. She was beautiful. Her long black hair spread across the red comforter. With each breath her breasts rose and fell. Using her elbows and feet, she scooted further on the bed so she lay crossways.

Eyes dark with desire and hunger stared at him. "I love you," she whispered. It was the first time she had uttered the tender words. They touched his heart sending a tremor down his spine and straight to his toes.

The bed creaked as he sat upon it. He couldn't wait to make love to her. Hear her soft whimpers as he felt her body shatter around his.

Slowly, he parted her thighs and knelt between them. He couldn't believe this beautiful woman was his for all eternity. His fingertips pushed between the comforter and her ass, lifting and spreading her wider. His cock throbbed, growing harder as he placed its swollen head to her moist slit. With a slow thrust of his hips he pushed between her swollen folds. She was wet, hot, and all his.

Her mouth opened on a gasp. Her pupils dilated, large and dark. The swish of her blood beat louder and louder in his ears.

Fallon was lost to sensation. His touch—caress. The gentle rock of their bodies together moved in perfect harmony. He filled her completely, the motion slow and intense.

Heat simmered in his eyes, golden pools of fire, as he stared at where they came together. He pulled from her body and then thrust slowly inside her—watching.

"Tight," he growled. "So fuckin' tight, darlin'." He breathed deeply, scenting their musk mingling together.

The tendons constricting in his neck brought her gaze to the vein that pulsed below his skin. Her fangs burst in her mouth with a savage need to taste him, to mark him as hers.

"Do you know how sexy you look hungry and aroused?" His tone was breathless, exciting her further. "I can't wait to feel your body tremble with release, as you sink your teeth into my neck."

Her pussy drew taut sending shudders up her womb. "Adrian." Her plea came out a whimper.

She heard the intake of air he sucked in through clenched teeth. "What, baby?" He ground his hips against her making a rotation that nearly made her come.

"*Ahhh…*" She arched, clenching her inner muscles, attempting to quiet the storm building inside her. She wanted to ride the rising climax as long as she could.

"Damn that felt good," he snarled as his canines dropped so that they pierced his bottom lip. He slipped his hands from beneath her ass putting one and then the other on each side of her head as he leaned forward draping his body over hers.

Arms wrapped around his neck, she buried her face into the side of his neck, inhaling his masculine heat. His blood called to her as she stroked the vein lightly with her tongue.

Fallon felt Adrian tense and knew he was fighting his orgasm. His hips moved faster with his excitement. His breathing was labored.

"Do it," he groaned hoarsely. "Bite me."

When her teeth broke his skin he cried out. It was a beautiful male sound of pleasure. His body stiffened. His breath caught. The fiery feel of his seed splashing against the walls of her sex and the heady flow of his essence down her throat triggered her climax.

Heat waves rippled through her, touching every inch of her inside and out. She held on to him as her body squeezed his cock, again and again. When the aftermath began to ease she moaned low and sated. Lazily she swiped her tongue over the pinpricks at his neck. Then she released a heavy sigh of contentment.

Adrian rolled from atop her, gathering her in his arms and pulling her against his chest. Fallon couldn't remember when she felt so loved, so cherished. Even the pain of losing Christy wasn't as raw when Adrian held her close.

"You're thinking about your daughter." It wasn't a question. How he knew Fallon didn't know.

She fought back the tears misting her eyes. "Yes."

"I know it hurts." He squeezed her. "Just promise you'll give me a chance to make you happy." The plea in his voice made her love him even more.

It seemed silly to realize this now, but Fallon had never gone through the grieving process. "I never got to say good-bye to Christy, before Chavez consumed my world. When I escaped, revenge and running absorbed me."

"Then it's time." He scooted off the bed.

In mere minutes, he was clothed in a tight pair of jeans that hugged his thighs and a solid denim long-sleeve shirt. He was adjusting his black Stetson as she stood.

Quickly, she dressed in black jeans, a yellow T-shirt and boots to match his. "What are we doing?"

As he took her hand in his, leading her out the bedroom and down the hall, he said, "The White Mountain community is a magical place. You can feel the spirits of their ancestors walking the land. The Apaches believe you can speak to the dead. If you listen you can hear them."

As they entered the living room, Fallon could smell the scent of yeast and bread baking from the kitchen. Voices rose and fell behind the door. Adrian headed straight for the front door, opened it and ushered her through. The night air was cool. Sounds of crickets chirping and an owl hooting greeted them. The sight of Cougar surprised her. He tipped his hat to her, but didn't say a thing as his bones crackled and popped, his long black braid melting into feathers as he took the form of an eagle.

Adrian and Fallon shape-shifted into bird form and flew through the sky.

When they came to the sacred caves that Chavez had held Fallon captive in, Cougar started to descend. Before Fallon and Adrian landed, the man had a small fire burning. He sat crossed-leg before the flames and softly began to chant.

Adrian led Fallon to where the mountainside dropped off and she looked across the treetops and the beauty that was the White Mountains. The view gave the illusion that she stood so high above the land that if she raised her fingertips above her head she could touch the heavens. Adrian released her hand, kissed her gently on the cheek, and then stepped away.

The smell of the burning pine, the rise in Cougar's voice as she stared blindly across the countryside filled her with a serenity she had never felt before. A breeze caressed her face and the smell of baby powder filled her senses. The cloud formations before her shifted against the darkened sky. If she didn't know better she could have sworn she saw Christy's cherubic face. Fallon felt the wetness upon her cheeks as tears lightly fell.

"Oh, baby." Emotion caught in her throat. Pressure squeezed her heart. "I miss you so much." She pressed her palm to her mouth to choke back the strangled cry that begged to be released.

I can do this. Adrian was right. Good-byes needed to be said before she could go forward. Christy was gone. Nothing could change that.

Fallon gulped down a breath of courage and let her hand fall to her side. "I love you, mommy's angel."

The clouds shifted and the slightest of smiles touched Christy's mouth before a brisk wind whipped through the gauzy mass that dissipated, replaced by bright shiny stars that twinkled in the night.

"Good-bye," Fallon whispered.

When she pivoted she turned right into Adrian's arms, which folded securely around her. Within his embrace, she could see the campfire had been extinguished. Cougar was nowhere in sight. Only she and Adrian stood on the mountaintop.

Chin resting on the top of her head, he asked, "Are you okay?"

Was she?

The ache in her chest had lessened. Her tears had dried. The baby powder she had smelled was replaced with an earthy scent that was all Adrian as he surrounded her with his love.

She nodded. "Yes." Their eyes met. In time she'd be all right, especially with Adrian by her side.

Fallon angled her head to receive his tender kiss—a kiss that said forever.

About the Author

A taste of the erotic, a measure of daring and a hint of laughter describe Mackenzie McKade's novels. She sizzles the pages with scorching sex, fantasy and deep emotion that will touch you and keep you immersed until the end. Whether her stories are contemporaries, futuristics or fantasies, this Arizona native thrives on giving you the ultimate erotic adventure.

When not traveling through her vivid imagination, she's spending time with three beautiful daughters, two devilishly handsome grandsons, and the man of her dreams. She loves to write, enjoys reading, and can't wait 'til summer. Boating and jet skiing are top on her list of activities. Add to that laughter and if mischief is in order—Mackenzie's your gal!

To learn more about Mackenzie McKade, please visit www.mackenziemckade.com. Send an email to Mackenzie at mackenzie@mackenziemckade.com or log onto her Yahoo! group to join in the fun with other readers as well as Mackenzie! http://groups.yahoo.com/group/macsdreamscape/

Look for these titles

Now Available

Six Feet Under by Mackenzie McKade

Coming Soon:

Beginnings: A Warrior's Witch by Mackenzie McKade
Lost But Not Forgotten by Mackenzie McKade

He found her six feet under and unearthed a passion beyond their wildest dreams.

Six Feet Under
© 2006 Mackenzie McKade

Buried six feet deep is not what Private Investigator Charlene Madison, had expected when she agreed to meet an informant at New Orleans' most famous cemetery. Neither was encountering the devil himself when Devin Leduc rescues her, only to imprison her in his arms. She can't explain her attraction to him, especially once he reveals his secret.

After centuries of darkness, Devin has found his light. Charlene makes his body burn with desire, along with his temper when her penchant for justice and her stubborn nature lead her straight into danger.

Together they will unmask a killer and discover a love so fulfilling, nothing, not even death, will quench the flames of passion.

Warning: This title contains hot, steamy explicit sex, ménage a trois, and violence told in contemporary, graphic language.

Available now in ebook and print from Samhain Publishing.

Legacy bond them—betrayal will test them—but, love and a little bit of magic will keep them together.

Beginnings: A Warrior's Witch
© 2006 Mackenzie McKade

Gifted with both Berserka and Wicce heritage, Sabine wonders which legacy will determine her fate. A path of freedom and independence? Or will the Berserka curse tie her to one man, not of her choosing?

After his father's death, Conall returns to Scotland to take his rightful place as chieftain. Fate steps in and unleashes his hot-blooded lust on one obstinate woman resolved on defying destiny.

A forced marriage binds them. Desire and their animalistic nature draw them together. But someone is threatening to destroy the fiery love growing between them. Salt in the water, poison in the wine has everyone looking askew at Sabine, including her husband.

When the clan demands Sabine's death, Conall must choose between family and the woman he loves.

Warning, this title contains the following: explicit sex, graphic language.

Available now in ebook from Samhain Publishing.

Fly Away

Discover the Talons Series

5 STEAMY NEW PARANORMAL ROMANCES
TO HOOK YOU IN

Kiss Me Deadly, by Shannon Stacey
King of Prey, by Mandy M. Roth
Firebird, by Jaycee Clark
Caged Desire, by Sydney Somers
Seize the Hunter, by Michelle M. Pillow

AVAILABLE IN EBOOK—COMING SOON IN PRINT!

Samhain Publishing Ltd

WWW.SAMHAINPUBLISHING.COM